Other works:

Soul in Ink: The Memoirs of a Journalist

The Jawn 2.0: Philly's Unsigned Talent, 2001-2007

Please enjoy.

-Dame.

www.damoncwilliams.com

Chapter One

RANDALL Jenkins took his usual seat - in a booth by the window, facing Walnut Street - of Two Boots Cafe, one of the trendier eateries that popped up in University City, an area that connects the University of Pennsylvania with Downtown and the rest of West Philadelphia, the neighborhood in which Randall grew up.

For several consecutive Saturday mornings, Randall ate at Two Boots since the diner opened months ago, and it drew a very mixed crowd. from the uppity millennial types working at or attending UPenn to the denizens that lived in the nearby neighborhood, all seemed to gravitate toward Two Boots. It also attracted the more seedier types who wanted to be thought of as hip.

And as of late, Two Boots had also somehow morphed into a hang-out spot for rappers throughout the city. The eatery represented a safe zone of sorts for these emcees, a low-stress environment that served as a stop-through for those on shopping runs through Center City.

It was also a place Randall easily got attached to.

But Randall was anything but trendy. Randall's eyes slowly drifted from his clothing - brown Timberland hiker boots, dark blue jeans and a Brown Tommy Hilfiger pullover - to the interior of Two Boots to, finally, the dozens of faceless passersby that briefly appeared in the window of the cafe.

It wasn't that Randall felt his clothing wasn't sharp; it was just that he felt it was always the *same*, more like a uniform Randall grew so accustomed to donning that it became a second skin.

Even Randall's car, a later-year model Honda Accord, with the only after-market upgrade being a stereo system Randall had installed two years ago, was staid; plain. And though the outside world thought of his job as a newspaper reporter to be an exciting one, Randall knew it too became bogged down by an unimaginable, inescapable monotony that enveloped him every time he stepped foot inside the newsroom.

Randall got a better look at the people passing in the window. As he gazed outside and watched as the midmorning sun glistened off one of the university's many gleaming, glass-clad high towers, there was a couple, laughing, as they pushed a newborn in one of those newfangled tricycle strollers that looked built more for the trails than for Walnut Street; there was a man, jogging in place at the red light, doubtlessly checking his completed activity rings on his Apple Watch.

Time seemed to be moving in slow motion as more and more individuals briefly came into Randall's focus, such as the two young women leaving the campus bookstore, and an apparent argument brewing between an Uber driver and student.

Randall sighed. *All the same shit,* he mused silently.

Indeed, sameness seemed to permeate every corner of Randall's existence. Randall covered urban culture and crime for The Philadelphia New Times Herald - a paper which was nicknamed by the locals as the *Philly Times*, and as such, Randall was invited to just about every concert, party and event.

Randall was also the de facto 'hood' reporter for the paper, meaning that if anything, usually something bad, happened in a black or brown neighborhood, he was usually the first reporter sent.

And more often than not, Randall was the *only* reporter sent.

But as well-known as Randall might be, he never felt more alone and disconnected from society at large as he did at that very moment, sitting alone, in a booth in Two Boots.

He felt a pang of jealousy toward the people in the window, wishing for an instant that he could be them, or, at the very least, be as happy and full of life as they seemed to be.

Randall's train of thought, which had no destination, was interrupted by Joshua "Seven" Anderson, a second-year student at the University of the Arts who worked at the diner and created mind-blowing art for posters and album covers to pay his way through school.

As Randall has now become a regular at Two Boots, the two have struck up a friendship: Randall would sometimes mentor Seven, and Seven was always eager to talk to the "hip-hop critic" to get Randall's thoughts on everything from the commonplace neighborhood cipher rhyme battle to emcee so-and-so's latest mixtape.

Randall thought that Seven always hipped him to "what's poppin'" in the hopes that Randall would put him in the weekly hip-hop column he wrote for the paper. Randall didn't mind; he actually admired Seven's hustle.

This time, Seven showed Randall his most intricate work yet. It was an album cover for a local artist, with the name of the album, "Bottom's Up," stylistically detailed inside a larger rendering of and upside-down Philadelphia skyline.

Randall thought it was a clean depiction that pushed the bounds of Seven's creativity.

"That's pretty ill," Randall said. "How much did you charge Estobahn for it? I like how you're coming along with the custom fonts and fade work." Estobahn was one of the more abstract emcees on the local circuit, one who mostly rhymed about issues such as Black Lives Matter and the inherent value of voting.

Randall always thought Estobahn's lyrics to be esoteric in an historical, scientific way - a welcomed breath of fresh air from the usual tired and played-out gangsta rap currently plaguing the airwaves.

Randall often found himself in spirited debates with those types of rappers, and he would always call out the 'four pillars' he thought responsible for the despicable present state of hip-hop music and its accompanying culture: the rappers who rhymed about that bullshit, the labels that pressed and promoted it, the radio stations that played it and the customers who purchased and streamed it.

To Randall, each of the four shared in the complicity, and each deserved scorn and rebuke; they were all at fault for what Randall deemed a cultural bastardization and an altogether ugly mutation of the true culture of hip-hop.

In fact, Randall would always call out those entities every time he was invited as a guest on some hip-hop or cultural insight program.

It was no wonder that Randall was adored by the backpack hip-hop crew, begrudgingly respected by the street emcees - and hated by radio deejays and programmers. Randall often sadly chuckled to himself whenever he recalled that it has been many months since his last radio show invite. Oh well.

"Nah, I did this on the strength. He's going to put me on when he gets put on. And besides, I get to sign my work and other people will see it; it'll go into the portfolio, anyway. It only took me about a week to hook up. And we all know Estobahn doesn't have any money. Do you really like it?" Seven always sought affirmation from Randall, and Randall, this time like most times, obliged.

"I think it's your best work yet," Randall said. "I'm telling you, if I ever write a book, I'm going to want you to do the cover for it."

Seven beamed. "Whenever you're ready. I already have a hot design in mind for that. But check it out homeboy, I know you didn't just come by so I can show you my latest layup. You want your usual?"

Seven had a real light and lively style about him; an attitude and outlook on life that Randall believed was the very antithesis of his own. The pang of that realization lingered for a few brief moments.

"Yessir. Turkey bacon fried a little stiff, toast, eggs scrambled dry and some grits, with coffee and juice in front."

Seven always smiled when Randall ordered his meal in that sort of old-school oddball way, and aptly ventured back to the kitchen to delegate to the dayside chef the details of Randall's order.

Seven is going to make that graphic arts degree pay off, even if it kills him, Randall mused to himself, as he went back to staring out the window. *Shit though, he's doing better right now than most of these hip-hop cats trying to make it.*

As with Estobahn, Randall lumped Seven into the group of local emcees and contributors that actually tried to push the creative bounds of the culture in more of a positive manner. Not like the sambo-ass, pseudo-playa rappers out today, who only rapped about misogynistic forays, absurd consumerism and attaining the very heights of the drug-dealing world, all the while venting misplaced anger.

Worse than that, Randall was of the mind that today's rappers lacked the general wordsmithing skills of hip-hop's founding fathers; and most damning in Randall's Judgment, he concluded that these sorts of rappers were doing material harm to the inner-city communities that seem to embrace this self-same negative music.

Randall simply grew angry at first, but lately he became enraged and incensed by what he was seeing as a devolvement of the culture; *his* culture. To Randall, these rappers were glorifying the very things that have and continue to hold black people back.

Sure, Randall was a fan of Wu-Tang Clan and Boot Camp Click, and he could stomach a little Biggie. *But at least they had talent,* Randall thought, still looking out the window while briefly ignoring his faint reflection in the diner's otherwise crystal-clear window. *And they could rhyme. Not this mumbling, stupid shit that's out now.*

Randall tore himself from those thoughts and propped open his MacBook Air. On it was all of Randall's work, as he has taken a liking to working outside and way from the newsroom. But on this unseasonably warm autumn morning, Randall was presently concerned more with the music on his laptop than anything else.

Browsing through his vast catalog of more than 20,000 songs - more than 40 gigabytes' worth, which were broken down into genres and sub-genres, Randall would minutely pick through and sort his collection with a maniacal obsession. After all, there was a lot of music in there, from Abba and Akinyele to X-Clan and ZZ Top.

Oddly for him on such a tranquil Saturday morning, Randall chose "Ante Up," by M.O.P.; the version with the Funkmaster Flex intro.

And just as that unmistakable electric guitar rift faded in - the signature sound of an all-time classic street anthem - a figure Randall had never seen before seemed to suddenly appear.

Randall didn't notice the door open, an odd miss, since he was seated in a way in which he could at least see the comings and goings of everyone in the sparsely occupied diner, but Randall did manage to catch sight of him maybe a footstep or two away.

When Randall looked up into the stranger's face, he noticed a deep, yet thin and very straight cut going down the right side of his face. The scar began right below his hairline, travelled through his eyebrow and continued its linear path that bisected his eyelid and eyelash, before resuming its wicked and determined path at the top of his right cheek and ending just below his jawline.

That, coupled with the stranger's other facial features: dark-skin, clean shaven save for a perfectly sculptured goatee, a small afro with no fade and one very small and shiny black faceted diamond stud in either ear, gave this stranger a mischievous yet supremely confident air about him.

When Randall's eyes meet his, the stranger gave a peculiar smile that curled the corners of his mouth and slowly unfurled across his face. Not quite an open-mouth smile but something more than a grin, and Randall noticed the top of what appeared to be a sparkling platinum toothcap.

His attire belied the warmth outside. He wore a partly zipped-up, black butter-leather bomber, black baggy jeans, tan nubuck Timberland boots and what looked to be a black Polo pullover. He then took the open seat to Randall's left.

The seat was already pulled back from when Randall first sat there but decided to move to his present chair, so the stranger was able to slide his lithe frame into the chair with ease.

"You don't seem the type to bang M.O.P.," the stranger said with a voice that had the strong accent of a place that Randall couldn't conjure. Randall, the son of a Caribbean-born father, has been around island culture, in some form, for most of his formative life, and it slightly unnerved Randall that he couldn't fit this stranger's voice with a particular island.

And in his professional life, Randall encountered people from all across the globe, and he was able to at least tell which continent someone was from. But this stranger's accent was brand new to Randall's ears. "You look more like the Arrested Development type."

Randall was seconds away from checking this stranger for the off-handed quip. Just as Randall was about to launch a protest to defend his lifelong love of "real" hip-hop, the stranger smiled.

"Man, I'm just fuckin' with you. Don't mind me; that's just my way. My name is Marcus."

Randall didn't long for nor need many friends, and certainly didn't have the space for a new one, especially a shit-talker who is obviously from out of town. But, feeling a bit quartered with his computer gear out and breakfast on the way, Randall reluctantly obliged Marcus.

"Yeah what's good. My name is Randall. And to let you know, my music collection is that shit," Randall said. "I only rock with the best. Don't mind me asking, but you aren't from around here, are you? Many of my folks are from the islands; you from St. Vincent?"

Marcus slightly tilted his head, yet it seemed his scar didn't move. His smile remained frozen in place.

"No, I've been around. Moved here just a while ago. Thought I'd get out and see what Philly had to offer. So, what else you got in there?"

Randall could talk religion, music, sports, weed, politics and all sorts of current affairs with the best of them, so he warmed up to Marcus' inquiries into his musical taste.

Seven appeared with the orange juice and coffee just as Randall was sizing up his collection to Marcus.

"Hey Randall, the cook said it would be about 30 minutes for your food, and that he's sorry to hold you up. Said drinks are on the house. Can I get you something else?"

Randall turned to Marcus.

"Hey man, you want anything?"

Marcus smiled, but otherwise didn't answer.

Randall then turned back to Seven, whose usually affable expression was now replaced with a mask of concern.

"Bring this dude a soda, Seven. And thanks for the head's-up about my grub."

Seven only nodded and retreated back to the kitchen.

Before Randall could continue his conversation with Marcus, the door to the diner swung open in a most elaborate manner, causing both Randall and Marcus to simultaneously look up and at the door.

Streaks, a flamboyant rapper from North Philly known for his over-the-top braggadocios in rhyme and lifestyle, entered the diner, twirling his car keys while chatting loudly on his iPhone.

"Yo Seven, let me get that porkroll sandwich and some coffee, bruh; these bitches got me tired," Streaks yelled to Seven, who was well within not-yelling range. "Make it strong."

I can't stand this motherfucker, Randall caught himself thinking, and was immediately ashamed of himself for such a rash and uncontrolled thought. It wasn't in Randall's nature to hate, but if there were anyone deserving a dose of scorn and admonishment, it was Streaks.

Because Streaks epitomized everything that Randall abhorred.

Streaks was a member of North Philly's "supergroup" Gravytrain, which used the collective funds from its various hustles to promote their artists through regional concerts and monthly mixtapes.

As Gravytrain was largely made up of hustlers trying to be rappers which led to a revolving door of various members serving time, coming home to record, fucking up and being sent back up-state, only to come home again, Streaks somehow was able to escape any real drama with the police and with rivals on the street, although rumors in certain circles were that Streaks was somehow protected on-high, which allowed his small yet enterprising drug game to flourish.

Randall continued to eyeball Streaks through his peripheral vision.

Streaks, light-skinned and wearing a blue, red and white terrycloth Fila sweatsuit with matching Fila kicks, seemed to go out of his way to floss as much as possible. Randall couldn't help but notice the gleaming platinum and diamond-encrusted Gravytrain logo, weighing down the matching platinum Figaro link chain.

A crispy white T-shirt provided the backdrop for Streaks' chain and pendant, one even Randall had to admit was nice, as it was a play on the old-school "Soul Train" logo, but with a Broad Street Line subway train serving as the centerpiece, with "North Philly" scripted at the top and "Gravytrain" scripted on the bottom hemisphere.

Still, Randall couldn't help but loathe Streaks' entire persona. Although never mentioning him by name, Randall often would refer to rappers such as Streaks when discussions turned to negative emcees.

Streaks and Randall even once had a staredown due to Randall's reluctance to give Gravytrain an exclusive play in the paper. Randall would mention Gravytrain's shows and new releases but refused to interview either singular members or the group as a whole.

Gravytrain wasn't the only group that Randall didn't touch; some groups were just too hot on the street for all the wrong reasons, and it's been more than once that Randall received a call from the police regarding a rapper he wrote about.

And Randall just didn't need that, so while remaining cordial, he wouldn't go out of his way to feature them in the paper.

Streaks took offense and appeared to want to get physical; but although quiet, Randall was nobody's slouch and was not about to back down.

Besides, Randall knew that assaulting a journalist is a state crime, and the residual fallout from some sort of altercation would have been a bad look, even for the well-connected Streaks. Coming to blows, or worse, with the only hip-hop reporter in the city would have consequences that Streaks didn't want. While not a snitch, Randall would put the entire weight of the paper behind crushing Streaks.

Randall continued eyeing Streaks as Seven brought out his coffee, a gaze only broken by Marcus' voice.

"You really don't like him, I can tell. Who is he?" Marcus asked in low, bottomless voice.

Before Randall could answer, Streaks gulped down the last of his coffee, and in one fluid motion, Streaks ignored his pork roll breakfast, slapped a sawbuck on the table, disconnected his call and was about to leave before he turned his attention to Randall.

"No shit. Hip-hop's Peter fuckin' Parker, out getting some sun. What's up, penman? You coming to our show tonight at Jeronimo's, or you're gonna go watch those backpack-ass rappers downtown? Gravytrain's going to tear some shit down, as always."

Seven then brought out Randall's food, and paused on his way back to the kitchen to catch the banter.

"Last time Gravytrain 'tore some shit down,' your man got carried out of that purse battle at the Plateau," Randall said, referencing a $5,000 round-robin freestyle rhyme challenge that one of Gravytrain's emcees was the odd's-on favorite to win, but would up being carted out, unconscious, after throwing knuckles with a heckling rapper in the crowd. "And anyway, y'all dudes too busy with that gun shit for me. But I did give it a proper layup in this week's article."

Marcus' smile deepened with Randall's strong yet diplomatic response. Streaks' took a step toward Randall, but in a non-threatening manner.

"Listen my dude. That thing with Red Flame was small, and had I been there, *none* of that shit would have happened," Streaks said, patting a small bulge protruding from the right side of the waistband of his sweatsuit. "Trust me, those bums are too light for us, either on stage, in the club or in the streets. They can have it however they want it. Come out tonight night and see for yourself, penman."

With that, Streaks put his phone back to his ear, fished his car keys from his left pocket, and began to walk out to his truck which was parked illegally in a handicapped spot and just a bit askew of the curb directly in front of the cafe.

And then Streaks did something that only reinforced Randall's simmering hate of everything Streaks embodied.

Accessing a small device on his keychain, Streaks' whip - a pristine Mercedes Benz G550 truck, replete with 24-inch rims and Yokohama low-profile reinforced tires - hummed to life, immediately blaring Streaks' latest song, "Death Undone."

Now less than five feet away from his sparkling SUV, Streaks stopped to admire his reflection being relayed back to him off his truck's custom iridescent paint job. After patting down the waves cresting throughout the hair on his scalp, Streaks took a quick glance up and down Walnut Street before landing in the leather-wrapped driver's seat and rocketing off.

One day, that dude is gonna get fucked up, and it's going to be bad, Randall thought, suddenly disinterested in his now-cold meal and lost in the vision of Streaks meeting a gruesome end. *That flashy shit and those rhymes are going to catch up to him.*

Randall also momentarily lost thought of Marcus, but quickly refocused on his new acquaintance who was still sitting there, smiling in an eerily unassuming way.

"That dude. He seems like he's just asking for some shit to happen to him," Marcus said. And for the first time, Randall could discern a slight glisten in Marcus' eyes.

There was certainly something strangely familiar about Marcus, but Randall just couldn't put his thumb on it. "But yo, why don't we hit up - what's that spot, Jeronimo's? - tonight, and check that show? Shit could be interesting."

Fuck that, Randall immediately thought. He had no plans at all of going to that show, and he had even less of a plan of going there with some stranger he had only just met. The club itself was located in a seedy section of North Philly, near 22nd and Dolphin Street, and as streetwise and well-known as Randall was, he knew he wasn't above getting wrapped up in some bullshit.

Jeronimo's had been shut down several times for various ordinance violations, and there have been more than one assault and one shooting to occur there.

Jeronimo's could double for a split-level trap house, if not for the lights, banners and parking lot up the block.

All in all, it just wasn't Randall's type of venue, and although he had been there before, Randall needed a very good reason aside from witnessing a Gravytrain set to get him to go.

Marcus sensed Randall's apprehension.

"Man, if you're tense about the atmosphere, don't worry about that shit. We'll be fine," Marcus said. "I know you've been there before."

Randall didn't appreciate such an intrusion into his thoughts nor the insinuation that he was somehow fearful of going. A little slight at just under six feet tall and 155 pounds, Randall, however, wasn't a lightweight in his own right, and knew well how to handle himself.

Still, Randall had to admit that Marcus had a point, as above all else, Randall valued self-preservation; the risk just didn't seem worth it.

While still leery, Randall told Marcus he'd think about it, and gave him the address.

"You know how to get there? I know you're new and all. It can get a little rough around there if you don't really know your way around."

Marcus' smile widened by half, but almost imperceptibly.

"I'll find my way there. And like I told you, don't worry about any drama."

Marcus got up as silently as he sat down and patted Randall on the shoulder. "See you tonight, homeboy."

Randall watched as Marcus followed a woman out of the diner, sliding through the closing door left slightly agape by the exiting patron. Although clear and bright outside, Randall couldn't tell in which way Marcus went after leaving the diner.

Randall sat there and pondered his new associate. Shaking his head as if to free himself from those thoughts, Randall sipped the last of his coffee and packed up his computer and prepared to leave. Just then,

Seven brought out the check.

"Not hungry this morning?" Seven asked, before joking that Streaks can make anyone lose his meal.

"He certainly turned my stomach. Him and that dude made for a strange morning."

Randall then put a $20 on the table to pay for his untouched meal, told Seven to keep the change and left.

As Randall exited, the look of concern deepened across Seven's face as he looked at the empty coffee cup and glass of soda, while pausing at the unsipped soda Randall ordered.

I hope everything is alright with Randall. He's a good dude after all, Seven thought. *His job must be fucking with him.*

Chapter Two

BY the time Randall reached his apartment on 35th Street in the tiny subsection of West Philly known as Powelton Village, his mind was flooded with thoughts of his strange, new acquaintance. It wasn't that he made a new friend, although given Randall's introverted nature, was strange within itself.

No, something else was bothering Randall, something he couldn't quite pin down. Something in Randall's mind was more out of place than usual.

Just as he pondered the source of his dismay, Randall's cell phone rung, which startled him, as it always did. Randall didn't receive nor expect a lot of calls on the weekend, save for irate weekend edition editors or a copydesk clerk needing some clarification.

Randall's friends were few, just how he liked it. This was a well-chiseled behavioral pattern that took decades to craft. Randall had come to accept the downsides of living such a lifestyle; in fact, Randall was growing to like and appreciate his inclosing solitude.

Randall glanced down at his phone, which the caller ID read "DJIV."

That could only be one person, and Randall felt a spring in his heart for the first time since waking up that morning.

"Hello?"

"Hey sweetie. Miss me?"

Ivey Stewart's voice was melodic, charming and easy going, just like her nature. Ivey has been Randall's girlfriend, although he hated that term. They enjoyed more of a steady relationship for several years now, and he was with her last night at the open mic on Passyunk Avenue.

Randall always thought highly of Ivey's sex appeal and matching intellect, and she was the only person privy to Randall's most sacred and innermost thoughts and fears.

When Ivey graduated from Drexel University a few years ago with a degree in Digital Music, she was hired as the Philly rep for Technics; a position, coupled with her live weekly sets and podcast, that catapulted Ivey to O.G. status throughout Philly's urban music scene. But Ivey never boasted about herself; she would rather play things as low-key as possible, which perfectly matched Randall's introverted M.O.

Ivey didn't lack admirers, but always managed to keep them at arm's length.

That was another thing Randall liked about Ivey; they were in agreement when it came to privacy; the more of it, the better.

Ivey and Randall often held intimate and lively, yet amicable, debates until the early hours of the morning, reasoning on matters as trivial and inconsequential as which leaf is better for rolling the best marijuana, to issues as deep as the world ramifications of the most recent war in the Middle East and the United States-Mexico-Canada Agreement.

"Of course. Sorry for not calling this morning." After driving Ivey to her duplex apartment in Fairmount and then making it back to his spot, it was already nearing daybreak, and he was too tired to make the call alerting Ivey that he arrived safely, especially after drinking entirely too much at the club the night before.

Ivey often hated it when Randall didn't call, but she wasn't looking to complain. She had other things on her mind.

"You're coming to see me spin at Decimal tonight, right? I have the entire set tonight because Liks won't be in."

Ivey was a hugely popular deejay on the circuit, one of the few female deejays known to spin solid sets and to defeat seasoned male deejays in turntable battles.

Ivey kept it light and breezy with Randall but loved him passionately.

Of all the people in Randall's life, Ivey was the only one he truly connected with and trusted. Randall met Ivey at a weekly B-boy set that she attended shortly after her graduation, and they have been an item, to one degree or another, ever since.

"You know I have to see my baby do her thing. But dig it, I might get there a little later; I promised someone I'd check out Jeronimo's tonight." Randall had hoped that Ivey wouldn't be pissed off; not so much about going to a different event besides her own, but about him going to such a seedy spot, period. Ivey often pleaded with Randall to not go to such venues, especially Jeronimo's, always carefully reminding Randall of his own brush with gunplay several years ago. "I'll come through about 11. Is that cool?"

Ivey hated not having her man at the top of her set, but she learned a long time ago not to argue when Randall said he was going somewhere or going to do something. Space was something Randall enjoyed, and Ivey didn't mind giving it to him, especially when Randall had to clear his mind or needed time to think after covering and writing about a particularly bad event. And lately, those types of bad-event stories were beginning to pile up.

Randall often made the reporter mistake of mentally bringing a lot of his work home with him, which lead to a buildup of emotional distress and depression; Randall hadn't quite mastered the art of leaving stories where they were after his shift was over.

Ivey took it upon herself to relieve Randall of as much stress as possible. So, if he wanted to go to Jeronimo's, then Ivey was cool with that.

Still, she worried about him. To the casual man on the street, Randall may look like somewhat of a soft target, but Ivey knew that when provoked, Randall is less than likely to cower, no matter the location or situation. Ivey knew that if enraged enough, Randall would abandon all thoughts of what may happen to himself in a skirmish and would be focused entirely on inflicted pain; she has seen that side of Randall before.

"That's cool, baby. Who you running with? I hope you haven't been making any new lady friends on the side."

Randall loved Ivey's playful jealousy, but he also knew that Ivey had nothing to worry about in the way of him stepping out on her again.

If anything, Randall has been overwhelmed lately with thoughts of losing Ivey. *The tables will soon turn on that,* Randall often repeated to himself, steeling his nerves for what he believed to be the inevitable.

"Nah, some dude named Marcus came through the coffee shop today, and he wanted to check out Gravytrain, so I said I'd meet him there. He said he's new around the way, but his face looks familiar."

"Okay; just make it there before my set's over. You're still spending the night, right? I haven't gotten next to you since last week, so have that stroke ready."

Randall felt a spasm tingle his genitals, a familiar response to Ivey's fresh talk. "No question baby; I'll be there for you and ready for you after that."

After he disconnected with Ivey, Randall disrobed and plopped down on the edge of the bed before stretching out. *Damn, Ivey is fine; and her brown ass is lovely.* Randall had to chuckle at the thought. But it was true, for Ivey Stewart was a work of dark-chocolate beauty. She stood at 5'9'' and rocked a tight natural hairstyle that framed her almond-shaped face and eyes to perfection.

Her face, mild and soft, contained stark signatures of her Caribbean heritage; full cheeks and lips, bright teeth and piercing pearl-black eyes that seemed divinely matched to her maroon-hued complexion.

Voluptuous, curvy, and possessing a high level of sensual adequacy, Ivey had the knack for instantly arousing Randall, making him forget about his woes and sexing his drama away.

Like last time.

Randall closed his eyes and thought back to last Tuesday, when he picked Ivey up after her set. She had flames in her eyes, and Randall knew right then that they were going to fuck.

Not make love, as that was reserved for wining weekends, Ivey often kidded Randall.

Tearing his mind from his last intimate encounter with Ivey, Randall shook the thought of Ivey and her overwhelming sex appeal. Instead, Randall got up and headed for the bathroom.

Randall took a long, hot shower for the second time. Randall high on hygiene, would take three showers a day. Randall hated even the remote feeling of being dirty; being so was just another reminder of his destitute upbringing.

As he dressed, he thought more about his new friend, Marcus.

It wasn't anything outrightly strange about him, but something continually nagged at Randall's mind, a feeling of uneasiness and uncertainty, something akin to someone's Spidey Senses warming up.

Mainly, it was the way Marcus looked at him, and how it seemed as though he could read Randall's mind, or at the least, his emotions. That bothered Randall because, above everything, he was sure to keep his emotions in check. Randall lived by the principle of the poker face and iron mask.

Randall's disposition was diametrically opposed to the idea of making new friends or of establishing stronger connections with his current roster of associates, outside of Ivey.

Ever since one of Randall's close friends admitted to sleeping with a girlfriend of his back in his college days, Randall always believed that he, himself, was his best, and only, friend. That, combined with being let down by so many fair-weather friends in the past, contributed to the way Randall dealt with people, which meant maintaining the very minimum contact necessary to not outright offend, but in a manner that afforded Randall the luxury of dictating the depths of any relationship.

Of far greater importance, Randall ignored that true warning sign festering in his gut, that feeling that urged him to stay as far away from Marcus as possible. It was the same feeling Randall experienced when he stepped out on Ivey, only to get caught by her with Tamara, a college radio show host that somehow caught Randall's eye.

Ivey long ago forgave Randall for that faux pas, but Randall hasn't forgiven himself. It was then that Randall promised to himself that he would always go with his gut reaction, no matter what, especially when dealing with people he scarcely knew.

After dressing, Randall dueled with the thought of not going as he again checked his e-mail, something of an every-hour habit, born out of the notion of always being in communication, something drilled into Randall's mind by his hard-charging editors.

Even on the weekends, Randall was generally on-call for serious breaking news and likewise, was perpetually wound tight when it came to his gig.

Still toying with the thought of not going to Jeronimo's, Randall relit a half-burned Garcia Y Vega blunt when an e-mail from Randall's features editor popped up. Right then, Randall knew he had little choice but to go to Jeronimo's after all.

Josephine Morgan served as the features editor of *The Philly Times*, and as pop-oriented as she was, she had little knowledge of hip-hop, especially the local variety. She was excited to have Randall on staff, and her e-mail suggested that going to the Gravytrain show would be a good chance to get background for a story on inner-city hip-hop spots. Not to do any hardcore reporting or writing; just go there, see what's going on and make mental notes for a future article.

Grabbing his keys, Randall was almost certain that he'd have nothing good to say about Jeronimo's.

Jeronimo's front walkway was packed more than usual when Randall made his way past the developing rhyme ciphers and clouds of strong-strain ganja that clung to the drab canopy. Several in the crowd were rappers themselves who knew Randall, and they exchanged fist bumps as Randall walked by.

As Randall stood by the lone emergency exit door halfway down the block, but still under the cover of Jeronimo's huge façade, he wondered why he even bothered to show up. Randall hoped to mask his uneasiness just enough to fly under the radar of the unknown hooded patrons and their menacing crews.

Fuck this, Randall muttered under his breath, trying not to lock eyes for too long with the many bloodshot stares he felt burrowing holes through his forehead. *I'm not going to get stuck up out here, just to see some bullshit Gravytrain set.*

Turning to leave, Randall noticed an approaching Marcus, who apparently parked on 22nd street.

Randall wondered if Marcus drove. He must have, Randall assumed, because Marcus didn't bother with knowing which Septa bus to catch.

Randall also figured Marcus could have walked from the Broad and Allegheny subway stop, but that was about a ten-block hike through a notoriously violent section of North Philly. It then dawned on Randall that he didn't know where Marcus lived. For all he really knew, Marcus could've lived around the corner from the club.

"Whatup cousin," Randall said to Marcus, who smiled at him. Randall noticed that Marcus had on black leather gloves and a vintage State Property leather bomber. Something was awkward with Marcus' gait. "You limping?" Randall asked.

Before Marcus could answer, the vibration of heavy bass emerged from the darkness. The approaching sound was unmistakable; loud and deep, yet with enough clarity to make out the lyrics. The vibration literally shook the pavement as it grew closer.

Randall turned to look.

Marcus didn't bother.

What the crowd first heard, felt and then saw, was Streaks' and his Gravytrain envoy of five whips, including Streaks' gleaming Benz. They were more than a block away and around the corner when the crowd first heard the squad. Streaks' truck was third in line, flanked by his generals both in front and behind.

Damn, that is one bangin'-ass system, Randall thought, hating himself for admiring anything at all connected to Streaks. But the true tone of the evening was set when Streaks and his entourage turned the corner.

It was as if Streaks' Mercedes bathed the entire strip in a white, icy-blue sheen.

Pushing the iridescent midnight black truck slowly up the street, the bass from Streaks' heralded set of 12 Sony XS-Series 20-inch speakers sent shockwaves through the gape-mouthed patrons. His twin pair of

Maxos blue-light halogen headlamps shone enough brightness that one could easily mistake the time of day as high noon, while the roof-racked PIAA lamps threw beams of light skyward, illuminating the broken-down second floor of Jeronimo's.

As Streaks and his fleet slowly made their way up the block, Randall's eyes briefly met his before Streaks resumed his player posture behind the wheel of his outsized truck.

After the cars turned right on 22nd Street to make their way to what served as Jeronimo's parking lot, Randall then returned his attention to Marcus, who was fiddling with his baggy jeans.

"Did you see that? Streaks is on some other shit tonight," Randall said, more out of amazement at Streaks' audacious posturing.

Marcus seemed enchanted by Randall's growing outward dislike for Streaks.

"Well, let's get up in this spot before shit gets out of hand out here," Randall said, motioning to the single door guarded by two huge, armed and angry-looking bouncers. "Just don't expect too much of a show from them Gravytrain cats."

Marcus smiled while still fiddling with his pants. "Oh, there will be a good show tonight, I can feel it."

The comment struck Randall as odd since he didn't pick up the sense that Marcus was familiar with Gravytrain, but he paid it little attention; instead, Randall pulled out the $20 needed to get in.

At the door, Randall received a rougher than usual frisk, while Marcus seemed to breeze through.

Once past security, Randall had to adjust his eyes to compensate for the thick clouds of marijuana smoke and exhaust from numerous lit Black 'N Mild cigars.

The cavernous club was dark, dank, and altogether imposing, with 40-inch club speakers perched in each corner, providing a circular enclosure for the packed bar and cramped stage. The disco lights were flashing intermittent globes of colors; glittering shards of red, blue and white-light hues danced off the shimmering jewelry worn by the patrons and their bottles of champagne and glasses of mixed drinks.

Randall's uneasiness was apparent.

"You don't like being in here, do you?" Marcus whispered in Randall's ear. For some reason, Randall thought it was more than just his darting eyes and unsure stroll that tipped Marcus off; little did Randall know, Marcus' intuition came from a deeper, darker source.

Randall didn't know the reason, but today of all days his resentment towards Streaks finally bubbled over, and it was indeed beginning to show.

"You need to lighten the fuck up some, Randall. Don't worry about Streaks and that bullshit earlier. I told you, you don't have anything to worry about."

Marcus threw back his head and laughed, his guffaw seeming to echo off the walls inside of Randall's head.

Randall could have sworn he spotted something that looked like a broken cross tattooed on Marcus' throat. "Unless you think Streaks' is going to jump off that stage at you."

As Randall considered the nature of his dislike for Streaks, the house DJ broke off the mix to announce that Gravytrain was about to take the stage.

Gravytrain had its full complement of members, and judging by their behavior, at least in Randall's mind, the crew seemed more menacing than usual.

Streaks grabbed the microphone before proclaiming, "Gravytrain is in the motherfuckin' house!" and took off the top to his baby blue Gucci sweat suit and then his contrasting undershirt, revealing an assortment of thug-related tattoos on his torso, including a large train with "Streaks" under it in bold script.

Streaks obviously had a thing for plush two-piece sweat suits, Randall thought.

Out the corner of his eye, Randall could see Marcus sneering and staring at the stage and towards Streaks.

Streaks and his Gravytrain crew spirited through their 45-minute-long set, with Streaks working the like-minded crowd into a frenzy. He, too, worked the women into a lather; his sex appeal evident by the screams of the adoring females.

Randall was even more put off by this undue fawning and mindless appreciation, while Marcus never tore his eyes from the stage.

With his pendant glimmering as it swung to and fro during his set, Streaks often clutched his frosty necklace to make a point.

The crowd seemed to love every verse of the nearly hourlong set. Marcus found it hilarious, but for an entirely different reason.

"Give it up for Gravytrain!" the house DJ urged, as a spent Streaks left the stage, with crew in tow.

An exhausted Streaks was seen heading toward the darkened VIP area, alone, when Marcus' smile grew even wider.

*****

DRIPPING with perspiration, an exhausted Streaks barely made it to the darkened, lonesome changing room that was situated right behind the greenroom. His vibrating cell phone was the only thing that broke his collapse into the tattered red leather sofa.

His pursuer, catlike, lurked several feet behind, his dark clothing blending in seamlessly with the shadows of the darkened corner he seemed to melt in to.

Streaks rubbed his eyes as he glanced down at his phone, which, along with the blinking "Exit" sign and the muted blue lights leading to the stairs and back to the stage, provided the only illumination in the cramped, dour-smelling room. *Not now,* an agitated Streaks thought to himself, hesitating for a second before deciding, on the third pulse, to answer the call.

"What the fuck do you want? I told you not to bother me when I'm performing." Streaks forgot for a moment whom he was talking to and caught himself a second too late. Streaks immediately regretted barking on his caller.

"You know exactly what I want," the caller said. "You think I give a shit about your show? There are bigger things going on; things bigger than you. We need to talk."

Streaks sat up on the couch, elbow on his knees, rubbing his head with one hand and holding his phone to his ear with the other. *They'll be a time when I won't need this motherfucker,* Streaks thought. *But until then, I better play by his rules.*

Streaks hated that his caller always made it appear that his music career was nothing more than a front - *something to do* - and that he looked at it as more of a hinderance to their arrangement than anything else.

Streaks' follower leaned further into the darkness, eavesdropping on the call.

"Can't this shit wait until the morning? I'm really not in the mood for any more of your requests. It was too close last time. We should wait before linking up again so soon."

Streaks really was not up to meeting with his caller ever again, but he knew he would ultimately have no choice but to eventually acquiesce.

"No, it can't wait. You fucking rappers always think things move on your time. You forget, you *owe* me for that time," Streaks' caller said. "Forty minutes, 26th and Jackson."

Before Streaks could protest, his caller was gone.

The figure in the shadows tightened his black leather gloves as his eyes glistened in the near-absolute darkness of the corner. He stepped as if in rhythm with the baseline reverberating through the club.

Streaks reached into his pocket and pulled out a pack of Newports before lighting one with his custom crystal-encrusted Zippo lighter. Streaks stared at it for a long moment before closing his eyes and leaning back into the splotched sofa and thought of his meeting to come.

A meeting Streaks would never make.

As he exhaled, Streaks thought of the debt he did indeed owe the caller. That debt allowed Streaks to be who he was - or whom he thought he was, considering the overweight persona that matched the overweight pendant now twinkling in the light of the glowing ember burning at the end of his cigarette.

Streaks chuckled to himself as he heard the faint drumbeat of one of his singles playing out on the main floor of the club.

I wish I never meet that dude. It's been nothing but trouble since. But it's too late to shake him now," a resigned Streaks thought to himself. *In too deep. But this will have to be the last time. Somehow.*

Streaks thought the *last time* was the last time, but he could tell that his caller needed him once again, and previously presented Streaks with such an offer that he literally could not refuse, and offer that Streaks was still repaying the interest on.

And Streaks had to admit his business affiliation, however much on the low, did allow for a certain freedom. A freedom that Streaks willingly embraced, knowing that this line of business was tantamount to a contact sport that bred only contempt and disloyalty; a gladiator playing field which had no stomach for the weak.

Streaks recalled whom - or what - he was, the days before making that faithful acquaintance with his caller. Back then, Streaks recalled rhyming more for the love of the art than for the money and fame that could someday come from it.

Back then, no one knew who Streaks was.

Something changed, though, when Streaks decided to mix games by parlaying the proceeds from his dimebag hustle into studio time and then into pressing up his own music.

But Streaks wanted more; needed more. And seeing other emcees get on by talking about the drug game, women and the quest for riches, Streaks concluded this was the only way to achieve all of his wants.

Streaks sighed. *That was the way, and there's no turning back now.*

With that thought, Streaks sucked in the last of his Newport, dropped it nonchalantly on the floor and stamped it out with the left heel of his still-crispy kicks.

As Streaks leaned back in the sofa, his pursuer took two long, silent strides, and within an instant, had overpowered Streaks from behind, wrenching the off-guard rapper's neck in vise-like chokehold.

The attacker managed to wrap Streaks' chain twice around the neck of the flailing rapper, and then performed several menacing, artery-bursting twists of the necklace, with every wrench of the chain causing both deep cuts in Streaks' neck and further cutting off his air supply.

Shocked, Streaks' tried in vain to fight back, but his attacker was just too strong.

His attacker could feel the life slipping away from Streaks, and as the dead rapper slumped to the floor, his attacker made sure the rapper was dead.

Spotting a loose spring in the tattered sofa, Streaks' attacker tore it from its base and leaned over Streaks' lifeless body. He then straightened out the iron coil and folded it in half until both sharp ends of the touched.

With a killer's uncanny strength and cool precision, he slowly thrust the points deep into Streaks' neck, bursting his jugular vein. Streaks' killer stepped back, smiling at the site of Streaks' blood pulsing from the hole in neck. The killer delighted in watching Streaks' blood slow to a trickle.

Before departing as stealthily as he arrived, Streaks' killer left a parting signature: he stuffed the bloodied Gravytrain pendant in Streaks' agape and blood-filled mouth.

*****

AS quickly as he disappeared, Marcus seemingly made an equally deft return, taking up his former position on Randall's right flank.

"So, what did you think of the show?" a smiling Marcus asked Randall. "I thought it was wack, but I was all for the finale'".

Randall had to agree. After all, even though to Randall, Gravytrain still rhymed about nonsensical bullshit, they did have the crowd going wild. Their fans were obviously happy.

But it was now past 11 p.m., and Randall knew he had to make it back downtown to catch the last of Ivey's set. Randall contemplated inviting Marcus back to Decibel but thought better of it. Marcus didn't seem interested in going anyway, as he was peeping two doe-eyed, light-skinned females outfitted in True

Religion jeans and shin-high Uggs.

"Yo, I need to be out. You good from here?" Randall hollered over the din of the rowdy crowd. Marcus nodded and followed him out of the club. Randall took a deep breath after stepping into the humid night air.

"I hope you enjoyed that thing. I'm out though. I have to see someone downtown."

The more he thought about it, the more Randall wanted to keep Marcus and Ivey as far apart from each other as possible. It was Randall's insecurities creeping up again. Although he was attractive in his own right, Randall couldn't shake the feeling that he just wasn't *fly enough* for Ivey.

Ivey's stature had raised her visibility, especially in the underground, where some of the dudes would openly hit on her or worse, attempt to touch her in ways not proper. Ivey never bought in to any of that game, but still, Randall wondered how long he would have Ivey.

Marcus smiled.

"Go meet your girl, man. I'm not going to hold you up. Ask her to spin up 'La Di Da Di,' a favorite of mine."

Randall could feel his heart hit the pavement as his knees buckled just a bit. *How could Marcus know about Ivey?*

Before Randall could put his thoughts in order, Marcus disappeared into the night, apparently already back inside the club. A bewildered Randall stumbled to his car, his mind racing over any plausible explanation that could calm his nerves.

As Randall got into his Honda, he called Ivey's cell. No Answer. *Of course, no answer,* a spooked and slightly annoyed Randall said to himself. *She's up in the booth.* His question would have to wait, as he glanced up at his rear-view mirror and noticed a larger than normal crowd gathering in front of Jeronimo's.

Not wanting to get caught in that, Randall disconnected from Ivey's voicemail and steered his sedan south on 22nd St. and turned right on Dauphin Street to avoid the crowded side streets to get back downtown; Randall decided instead to take Broad Street.

Randall left too early to notice that the crowd included police, stunned onlookers, a detective and a fast-moving, though somber-looking, paramedic unit.

Nowhere in the crowd would he have noticed Marcus.

Chapter Three

DETECTIVE Barron Wilkinson couldn't believe his eyes.

But as the paramedics carted Streaks' lifeless body through a stunned crowd and into a waiting ambulance, Barron was certain the events of the past few moments were no illusion.

Barron thought about who would kill Streaks in such a brazen and audacious manner as he stood midway down the alley from Jeronimo's; the detective was entirely caught off-guard by the current twist of events and tried to stay out of sight as he processed the scene as quickly as possible.

It was true that Philadelphia's murder rate was churning out of control with a spiraling body count and a string of bloodletting which left the nightly newscasts sounding more like a morbid death rollcall than reports on the latest civic occurrences.

And with the city's Black, brown and poor neighborhoods griped in a wave of fear of repercussions from killers if they dared talked to the police, whom many neighborhood residents considered the enemy as well, gunners and criminals seemed to operate at will.

Still, for Streaks to be killed in a venue with more than two hundred people inside, all of whom presumably knew him or of him, befuddled Barron. He was puzzled at how the killer, or killers, could move so stealthily through the crowd, commit the crime, and vanish in less than 20 minutes.

While in New York, the detective investigated all sorts of murders on the rap circuit. As one of the first members of NYC's infamous "Hip-Hop Investigation Unit," Barron was accustomed to getting in the weeds with so-called "street" rappers. And now, with more and more rappers trying to live up to their tough guy/drug kingpin stage personas, Barron knew this assignment in Philadelphia had the potential to catapult his work into the national spectrum of law enforcement.

And by the way his last assignment unfolded, Barron knew he needed every break he could get to right his stalling career.

In order to get where he wanted to go, Barron had to form bonds with the very same people he frequently pinched. It meant he had to sometimes deal with street-level hustler-rappers to gain info on those who were really behind the shootings that have recently plagued Philly's rap scene.

While in New York, Barron honed his dealings like a master craftsman, sharpening each connection into a well-defined, and often accurate, point.

It worked when Barron used a tip from a disgruntled rapper who flipped on the owner of a record label who was behind a firebombing of a club in Brooklyn; it also worked when the detective finessed a beef between deejays to find the culprit of a club shooting in Queens that left one patron paralyzed from the waist down.

And it was beginning to work in Philly, until a few minutes ago.

When Barron decided to take up the Philadelphia Police Commissioner's offer to head up Philly's own rap bureau, he was hesitant, but eventually jumped at the offer.

In reality, Barron had little choice.

After all, the detective spent several years and several thousand dollars building up his East New York network of snitches, turncoats, informants and other altogether salty individuals who had their ears to the street and info for sale.

It was a delicate dance that Barron had all but mastered, save for his last assignment; and when he left the Big Apple for the City of Brotherly Love, he found a prime partner is Streaks, who too knew how to dance the street tango.

But that partner was just carted out of the game, dead.

And now Barron was being challenged to learn a new two-step in one of the most unwelcoming of arenas and under the most severe of circumstances.

For some reason, Streaks had the bad habit of getting pinched for minor street-side offenses, like selling weed or driving without a license. Barron would offer Streaks a wrist-slap in exchange for info on various low-level pushers, individuals a step or two above him on the hustle ladder or a foe for whom Streaks had no love and gave zero fucks about.

Barron solidified their bond and Streaks' long-term cooperation when Streaks caught a gun charge a year ago that the rapper couldn't outright shake.

Word had it that Streaks was carrying one of his many illegal guns, this time a hefty, bright nickel-plated Desert Eagle XIX, along with three interchangeable calibers. Streaks couldn't explain why he had such a gun, why its serial number was filed off, nor why on Earth he would need chambers that would enable the gun to fire four different sizes of ammunition.

The get was a boon for the anti-gun task force and made for a considerable development in the world that contained only cops, rappers, rhymes and crimes.

But Streaks could tell Barron something else, something much more valuable; something that would make his gun charge all but disappear.

The streets were talking, and the rumors were that Streaks, desperate to stay out of jail, willingly flipped on a neighborhood rival that Streaks knew warehoused distribution-level amounts of heroin, fentanyl and marijuana, along with a cache of guns, in of one of his stash houses in the Kensington section of the city.

One thing that was quite clear to Barron was that Streaks would do whatever it took to stay out of prison, even if it meant breaking the long-held street code of never "dry snitching," or volunteering info to the police, even on an adversary.

The bust that Streaks' information led to simultaneously cemented Barron's stature and position within the Philly police department and instantly granted Streaks a free pass of sorts, something along the lines of diplomatic immunity on a 'hood level.

No one ever heard of nor spoke of the gun charge ever since.

That, in turn, freed Streaks to step up his hustle and fold his ill-gotten proceeds into his burgeoning rap career. Barron oftentimes looked the other way, as long as the juicy tips kept coming in.

And Streaks more than made sure those tips kept coming in, as he had no problem, moral or otherwise, in dropping dimes on his rivals and competition.

Barron wondered; had Streaks' informing ways gotten out and reached his many enemies?

Snapping back to the scene at hand, Detective Barron Wilkinson instinctively backed away from the still-shocked crowd, not wanting to be recognized by anyone he may have collared or flipped into a confidential informant. It would be more than awkward for either party if Barron were to be made on the scene of such a fresh murder.

"That's fucked up how Streaks was choked out," Barron overheard a hooded bystander tell another, between puffs of a freshly-lit Black 'N Mild cigar while shaking his head in that pitiful way one does when recounting a saddening moment that had minimal personal effect. "I heard the bartender broad found dude when they called for him to go back onstage. She came running from downstairs, screaming that someone killed Streaks."

"That's ill. I knew son had beefs, but that's crazy," Black 'N Mild's partner said, himself puffing on a marijuana-packed Swisher Sweet. "Choked out with his own platinum chain? That shit had to be gruesome."

Leaning just within earshot, Barron braced himself against the grimy stucco wall of Jeronimo's alley as he had to agree with the overheard assessment.

His years of training - through homicide and crime-scene analysis, cultural assimilation and special operations, tactics and negotiations - told him that he didn't need to see the killing floor to put the deathly sequence together. Regardless, the homicide department will gleefully provide Barron with the grislier details.

Streaks' murderer overpowered him, and with uncanny force, strangled the surprised rapper with his very own custom platinum chain.

Streaks never had a chance.

And even more telling, the killer apparently left a chilling signature, with Streaks' beloved pendant stuffed halfway down his throat.

I knew that heavy chain would be the end of him, Barron cynically said to himself. Barron always thought rappers, and Streaks was no different, spent way too much of their relative wealth on gaudy, obscene jewelry and out-priced cars, which Barron believed was a way for these rappers to overcompensate for their hollowness. The irony was not lost on the detective.

Streaks' murder more than complicated Barron's small, yet growing network. As this was certainly a case that fell within his jurisdiction, he knew he would get the call to lead the investigation.

What's more, the city was trying to crack down on inner-city killings, especially after the mayor's ambitious yet flawed anti-gun initiatives failed to take root in Black neighborhoods.

As if on cue, Barron's cell phone vibrated. The caller ID flashed "unknown," but he had no doubt about who was on the other end.

"Wilkinson," Barron whispered into his cell phone, slowly pacing his way further in the dark alleyway that ran behind the club. He had a bad sense that he knew what was coming.

"The captain wants your ass on his carpet at 7 in the morning," a no-nonsense voice stated. Barron didn't work with a partner, and that put off many within the department.

Other officers were often left forwarding and relaying his messages. Of course, a few relished the moments when the captain was furious with his lone wolf detective.

Especially Officer Timothy Jacobs, a three-year veteran of the force whose main duty was walking the Center City beat. On this night, Timothy was filling out paperwork when he was tasked with locating the detective.

Nature of the beast, Barron reinforced in his mind, before replying to Officer Jacobs. *If I were them, I'd hate me too.*

"What does Cammie want?" Barron asked, using the nickname for Captain Carmichael "Cammie" Fleming, the Irish born second-generation captain of the 19th precinct, one of the police districts in which Barron operated out of. The 19th was just one of the many city precincts where Barron had a desk. The aspects of his work mandated that Barron have a desk in the neighborhoods where most of the rap and club-connected shootings occur. In other words, in the Black, Hispanic and poor neighborhoods.

Peers were undoubtedly put off by Barron's apparent carte blanche.

Cammie was a straight-laced, hard-nosed captain that rose through the ranks and was proud to the point of boastful of his 31 years ("and counting") of service. Cammie was considered a stand-up 'officer's officer' for not implicating fellow cops during the MOVE bombing trial and, later, through the stripper scandal, which involved members of the state police.

Cammie was able to emerge virtually unscathed from each potentially career-decapitating fiasco, and he earned respect throughout the department as a result. His father, the first Captain Fleming, died 20 years ago after being mortally wounded in a wild shootout with a team of bank robbers in the Port Richmond neighborhood.

Cammie was known to have a particular disdain for flashy cops, and by the nature of Barron's work, he frequently felt the full brunt of the captain's wrath.

"He wants to know what you know about the murder of your latest informant. You know, the one you let go after he was caught with that Desert Eagle with the serials filed. Streaks. He was just murdered a few minutes ago, and crime scene called us."

Barron felt his bad situation worsening by the second.

"How did the captain find out so fast? And why didn't he call me first?" Baron asked, still creeping up the alley.

Timothy smiled as he imagined Barron itching on the other end. That itch was about to become a full-blown case of impetigo for the detective.

"Crime scene called here when they went through Streaks pockets, and along with a few dime bags of marijuana, two ecstasy tabs, a pack of Newports, $800 in cash, smashed sunglasses and his car keys, they found his cell phone. Any idea who his last incoming call was from?"

Oh shit, Barron thought.

"That's right, rap cop. Streaks' phone was still unlocked when the baggers zipped him up, and one of them recognized your number. And once the on-scene lieutenant got wind of it, he ordered it to be called it in."

"Streaks must've thought highly of you to have your number on his speed-dial."

Barron cursed himself for making the rookie mistake of not having a burner cell for communicating with informants. *Fuck.*

"Cammie was on his way out the door when the call came in, and he wants you to explain how your favorite stool nigger in the 'hood' could wind up dead no less than 20 minutes after talking to you."

Barron almost fainted, and not from Jacobs' racial epithet. Less than two years on the job in Philly, and his career was flashing before his eyes. Again. It was a brief flash, like a supernova on fast forward.

"So, is that it? Cammie just wants to see me before morning roll call?" Barron asked, trying to squeeze more info out of Jacobs.

He could envision Timothy licking his chops like a malnourished wolf on the other end.

"Yeah, one more thing. He said if he finds out you were at the club, he'll send your ass back to New York faster than air can move."

As the line went dead, Barron felt the sweat on his back go cold. He, too, was puzzled at how Streaks could be killed in such a way.

*****

AS Randall turned right off of Dauphin Avenue and onto Broad Street, he was having a hard time forcing his mind to focus on Marcus' uncanny intuition.

Zooming down Broad, by the Nation of Islam's North Philly mosque, past the Shriners' Hospital for Children and towards Temple University's main campus and dorms, Randall's thoughts were just as vague as the blurred facades of the buildings he passed.

Maybe I mentioned Ivey and her deejay set to Marcus, Randall thought to himself, although he was certain he hadn't. If there were one guarantee about Randall's persona, it was that he maintained strict secrecy concerning those involved with him on a personal, intimate level. Yet another painful lesson learned over the past few years.

Now crossing the after-midnight shadows of the Masonic Grand Lodge of Pennsylvania and City Hall at Broad and Market, Randall made a quick turn around the loop, and heading down Chestnut Street towards Decimal.

With Marcus' eerie remarks still on his mind, Randall pondered further when his cell phone vibrated, jolting him from his thoughts. The caller ID blinked "Editor."

Guiding the Accord with his left hand, Randall lifted the cell to his right ear. "This is Randall," was his usual way of answering the phone when someone from the paper called. It was one of the weekend editors, calling from the newsroom and sounding a bit too excited, given the hour of the call.

"We just got word over the police scanner that there has been a murder at some club in North Philly," Cameron Anderson said. "Somewhere around 22nd Street. Did you hear anything about it?" Randall certainly didn't hear about any murder, and his cell would be going crazy if something major happened.

"No, and I was just in North Philly and didn't see anything. Maybe it was one of those calls that come over the scanner that sound more dramatic than necessary. Or maybe it was just a neighborhood thing that had nothing to do with any club."

Randall hated minimizing any shooting, but Saturdays were one of his precious off-days, and besides, police public affairs would have all the details when Randall arrived for work on Sunday afternoon.

Another aspect of the job Randall loathed was that he seemed to always be the first reporter called when there is a shooting that could be remotely rap-related.

"We don't know the details yet but keep your ears open; you'll most likely have to follow it when you come in for Monday's paper."

Figures, Randall thought, as he ended the call. Immediately after Randall disconnected with Cameron, his phone vibrated once more.

"Baby! Where are you? Did you hear what happened?" A frantic Ivey yelled over the din of Decibel. She sounded legitimately petrified.

"I'm on Chestnut Street now, about six blocks from club," Randall said. "What happened?"

Ivey was yelling on the other line, barely making much sense.

"Someone killed Streaks at Jeronimo's! Can you believe that shit? The deejay just called from over there, saying the cops just rolled Streaks out of there and won't allow the few people still down there to leave."

Randall's grip of the Honda's steering wheel slipped as his cell phone fell from his hand, causing the car to swerve towards the curb at Fifth and Chestnut. Steadying his driving hand, he picked up his cell from the driver's side floor and put it back to his ear.

"Did you hear what I said? Someone killed Streaks!" Ivey was yelling at the top of her lungs.

"I heard you, but I just couldn't believe it. I just saw him earlier at the café', and then again at the club. Last I seen him, he made an exit, stage left, after rocking," Randall said.

It then dawned on Randall that this was the killing Cameron was talking about.

Randall could tell that Ivey was concerned about his safety, and that she was thankful that he didn't witness it, or worse, somehow got caught up in the drama.

"I'm okay though, good thing I left when I did, right?" Randall breezily offered while idling at the red light at 4th and Chestnut Street in Old City, somewhat soothing Ivey's tense nerves. At any rate, Randall was used to receiving calls about some murder, and by now had begun to react almost emotionless upon hearing the news. It was always the after effect of covering murders that would plunge Randall into a spiral of dismay, sorrow and anger.

He always knew that every now and then, Ivey needed some reassurances of his safety. Randall didn't mind. He actually loved that about Ivey. Randall would often call Ivey his guardian angel for how she always looked out for him and delivered timely advice.

"That's good. But from the way it sounds, the scene was out of control," Ivey said. "Anyway, I'll be outside waiting for you. My set is over, and the news about Streaks just makes me want to get up out of here."

Randall certainly didn't blame Ivey for her wanting to bounce. Besides, Ivey had every right to be suspicious of spillover drama.

As a deejay, Ivey has been in more than one seedy spot, and has witnessed her fair share of fights that have escalated into all-out brawls and gunplay. Just last month, she was wrapping up a set at Princeton Hall in West Philly when an angry rapper shot up the car of longtime rival.

It was becoming par for the course, sure, but such events have skewered Ivey's worldview.

Especially nowadays, when her man was usually one of the first reporters to cover those incidents and the fallout.

"See you in a second then, baby," Randall said, ending the call. Even though he wanted to quiz Ivey about Marcus, Streaks' death trumped all other inquires.

And as Randall's Honda approached the waiting Ivey, he could tell by her body language that she was in no mood to talk about Randall's new friend.

Standing there in her form-fitting leather hipster, camouflage cargo pants and brown-on-yellow shell-toe Adidas, Ivey looked just like the many hip-hop fans spilling out of the joint. Her throwback earrings, doorknockers with "Ivey" scripted through the center, sparkled in the shine from the streetlights.

She's always prettier than the last time I saw her, Randall thought to himself, as a relieved Ivey spotted him, waved, and made her way to the curbed Accord.

"Glad to see you, baby," Ivey said, kissing Randall on his cheek and settling into the passenger seat. "That news about Streaks freaked me out. When I was leaving, Chewy, the cat that spins after me on Tuesdays, told me that the cops from the 19th district had everybody that was at the club pinned up against the wall, frisking them and seeing if they knew anything. This shit is bizarre."

Bizarre indeed, Randall thought. *Bizarre that I managed to miss that.*

Ivey sensed Randall's vibe.

"Seems like you just missed Streaks' being killed. That's crazy. Did you see anything?" Ivey asked, taking off her jacket and turning on Randall's CarPlay system. She beamed her "official bootleg" of the new Jay-Z/Little Wayne album.

"No, I didn't see anything, but you know Cameron already called and pinched me to do the follow up when I get to the newsroom later. But Streaks seemed the same to me during his performance," Randall said. "He gave his normal show, you know, stalking the stage and stripping his shirt for his fans."

Randall's dripping sarcasm towards anything remotely involving Streaks wasn't lost on Ivey, but she paused at that comment and considered the moment.

Ivey always thought Randall could be cold-hearted towards people he didn't like, and if something evil befell them, then, to Randall, it was only a matter of comeuppance and karma universally working out.

Ivey, on the other hand, had a much larger reservoir of compassion, always granting people a slide while trying to understand their side.

"I know you were never a fan of Streaks, but even you can see he didn't deserve to go out like that. I mean, choked to death, and with his own chain? What kind of shit is that?"

"I don't know, but you should have seen the way his was flossing at the café earlier today. He acted like he had not a worry, floating through as if he were immune; maybe his street rep finally caught up to him," Randall offered in that clinical way that reporters often do, before hooking left off Bainbridge Street and down Second Street.

The overflow of young hipsters from South Street, the popular thoroughfare that ran parallel to Bainbridge, crowded the streets, causing traffic to slow to a crawl.

"Maybe. Whatever the case, I'm glad you weren't there to see it go down," Ivey said, before pointing to an open parking spot near the WaWa on Second Street. "Pull over, hon. We need a couple packs of Entourages."

After maneuvering into the parking spot, Randall and Ivey bounded out of the car and headed towards the 24-hour mini-market. Randall seemed preoccupied, grappling with the turn of fate that would cause him to somehow miss Streaks' murder, only to wind up being the reporter assigned to cover it.

Ivey, who walked in ahead of Randall, was now in the candy aisle talking to Mecca, another female deejay who had news on Streaks' murder as well. As Randall closed in, he caught the tail end of Mecca's animated retelling.

"Man, the fuckin' back room was covered in Streaks' blood. It looked like someone took a paintbrush, dipped it in his throat, and painted the room. It was awful, like what Bill the Butcher said he was going to do to young Vallon," Mecca said, shaking her head while digging her hand into a not-yet-paid-for bag of spicy Doritos.

Mecca always referenced movies while telling a tale, living for the dramatic effect. "I was at Jeronomo's all night, but a lot of people bounced before the cops even got there. I was up in the office, talking with the soundman and trying to roll my Backwood when the bartender girl came running up the steps. Her shrill-ass voice could be heard over the music, and I had to go down and see what the commotion was."

"You seen Streaks' Body?" Randall blurted out, wishing a split-second later that he hadn't.

"Oh, what's up Randall. Yeah, I saw Streaks' body. He was on the floor in the middle of a pool of thick, red blood. I almost threw up at the sight," Mecca said between nibbles of the cheesy chips. "I wouldn't wish that shit on my worst enemy."

Mecca had apparently beat the impromptu lineup as well and hopped the subway to make it back downtown.

Randall and Ivey slowly nodded their heads in agreement. No matter the beef, no one wanted to see anyone they knew mutilated in such a fashion.

"But that was one ill show, wasn't it, Randall?" Mecca said, wiping her orange-hued fingers on Randall's back. Mecca and Randall always played like sister and brother. The two have been friends long before Randall and Ivey hooked up; by happenstance, Randall and Ivey both knew Mecca, but Randall didn't know until very recently that Ivey and Mecca also had a long-established friendship. "I'm surprised you missed all that shit after, though."

"Lucky me," Randall said as he swiped Mecca's hand away. "I must've just left when that shit broke out. Me and this cat Marcus caught the Gravytrain set though. I thought the show was pretty much standard fare."

"Yeah? I seen you posted up by the door, looking like you wanted to be anywhere but there, but it didn't seem as though you were with anyone," Mecca said while fishing out a crumpled $10 bill from her purse. "You must've been out before that shit got bloody."

"Pink vanilla or natural?" Ivey yelled to Randall, throwing the decision to him of which flavored Entourages to purchase.

"Pink Vanilla," Randall said, before turning back to Mecca.

"You had to see the dude I was with. He had on a leather jacket, white kicks," Randall said. "We left the club together."

Mecca shrugged it off, not really caring about that minute point. "Yo, Ivey, can you give me a lift home? It's mad late, and I'd hate to have to catch the bus back up the way."

Randall stared at the back of Ivey's head and then back at Mecca, who was smiling the smile of a very high person. He knew right then he would be dropping Mecca home.

It was cool with Randall, though. Mecca was good people.

"No doubt, Mecca, but make sure it's good with Randall," Ivey said, turning to Mecca and Randall with the just purchased blunts. "You know how Randall gets about his whip."

"Yeah, like he's pushing a Beamer," Mecca kidded, slapping Randall on the back of his neck.

"I'd only drop your ass on the corner, Mec-Ho," Randall said, laughing. "You're used to working them streets."

Randall always enjoyed kidding around with Mecca, and at that particular moment, the brief levity helped to both soothe the news of the night and to provide a good façade for Randall, who was otherwise consumed with thoughts about Marcus.

After dropping Mecca to her apartment in East Falls, which, ironically, is about 10 blocks from Gravytrain's main recording studio, Randall could barely contain himself, wanting to quiz Ivey on Marcus. But Ivey would have her own inquiry tonight.

"So how was that show, really?" Ivey asked as they turned down Ridge Avenue. "That's strange that Mecca didn't see, what's his name, Marcus? I wonder if he made it home safely himself."

That was an interesting point, as Randall just now realized he never bothered to get Marcus' cell phone number. Randall was never the open-arms type, and if someone wanted to hang out with him, well, they would have to wait for Randall to call them. That's just how he rolled.

But when it came to Marcus, Randall thought that it was indeed strange that neither he nor Marcus offered each other their respective phone numbers, nor did either ask. For his part, Randall just didn't think it was a good idea at the time. And who knows what Marcus thought about the matter.

"I'd call him if I had his math, but I'm sure he made it out of there before the drama really set in," Randall offered as he cut over 22nd Street towards the Art Museum. "He seemed strange tonight. I mean, not like I know him all like that, but he seemed preoccupied with something. And when Streaks' drove up - you know how he liked to make an entrance - Marcus barely bothered to look up at him."

"What does that mean though? You barely paid Streaks any of your attention, either" Ivey countered while licking the broad ends of the Entourage leaf, deciding to leave the heavier dutch for their early-morning nightcap. "Since when do you care if someone is paying Streaks any attention? You were always of the mind that he got enough attention as is."

Randall was silent as he slid his Accord around Elkins Oval and across Spring Garden Street, taking a much more scenic route to Ivey's apartment. He knew that Ivey was most likely right; he was wasting too much time thinking about Marcus.

Still, there was one thing he had to know. And the way the feeling rose up his back, he had to know - now.

"So, this cat, Marcus. Remember I told you he had a familiar face?" Randall said in an even tone, careful not to tip off Ivey to his increasing leeriness. "Do you ever remember talking to some dude with his name? Dude has a wide-ass smile, but spooky, dark eyes. Short afro. Slice on the right side of his face?"

Ivey's eyes sparkled. *And I thought I was the jealous one,* she mused to herself, while smiling inwardly at Randall's play.

"Baby, you don't have to worry. I don't know a Marcus and a Marcus didn't try to hit on me," Ivey said, before lighting the flared end of the just-rolled blunt. "For all we know, Marcus beat the scene right after you did. And if he were there, then that's just another story he'll share."

Randall wanted to know the *other* story, the one that explains how on Earth Marcus would know Ivey.

Randall finally let it go.

"Baby, Marcus said he knew you, that you should play a favorite song of his," Randall said, plaintively as possible. "I'm thinking, did I mention your name to him, or where you spin at?"

Ivey giggled, tipped her head back and exhaled a bluish-grey smoke that temporarily blotted out the blur of the passing street lamps.

"Sweetie, you are far too suspicious. Here, have a puff," Ivey said sweetly, before passing Randall the blunt. "You aren't the only person that knows I'm a DJ. Marcus probably has friends who are deejays, and you know how the word spreads through the underground. And isn't that how you guys talk anyway? Don't sweat it baby. I'm sure it's an innocent type of thing."

Randall inhaled deeply before passing the Entourage back to Ivey. Randall wasn't so sure, but he let it drop when he pulled into Ivey's complex just above Fairmount Avenue. He decided that he wouldn't bring it up anymore tonight, but he knew, for his own mental health, he would need to find out exactly how Marcus knew about Ivey, one way or the other.

Ivey was clearly ready to move on as she prepared to exit the Accord. She had a mischievous glint in her slightly bloodshot eyes.

"Anyway baby, why don't you come on up, and I'll help you forget all about Marcus and Streaks," Ivey said before slowly sliding out the passenger side, giving Randall a full view of her curves.

Ivey turned and smiled, waiting for Randall to emerge. Randall always wondered how he lucked up into finding and keeping Ivey.

*****

IT was early Sunday morning. Very early.

Streaks was murdered less than eight hours ago, and although Randall and Ivey had yet to stir and start their day, Detective Barron Wilkinson was already at his desk. But this time, at his big desk at Police Headquarters, known with equal parts admiration and disdain as the "Roundhouse."

The morning sun had yet to crack the navy-blue horizon, which sparkled with the reflections of lights from neighboring office buildings.

This won't take long, Barron thought to himself as he rummaged through some files on his desk, trying not to draw the attention of the rank-and-file officers, who were no doubt puzzled to see the detective so early on a Sunday.

Barron finally found what he was looking for, and it was 6:15 when Barron whipped his black Chrysler 300 into the reserved parking space in the lot adjacent to the 19th District.

In a twist, Barron decided to dress as a straight-laced detective for his meeting with Cammie: two-piece suit, white button-down and solid tie.

Taking a deep breath, Barron exited his car and marched to Cammie's office, but the door was already open.

Barron's captain had company.

"Sit down, Wilkinson. You know why you are here. Now, tell me what I want to know, or things could end bad for you; worse than they did in New York," Cammie said, while looking Barron dead in the eye from across his withered walnut desk. "What did Streaks give you?"

Barron squirmed just a bit in his chair, unappreciative of his captain's tone, especially in front of a stranger. Worse was Cammie's pointed reference to the situation that drove Barron from New York in the first place.

It was officially written off as a generally successful end to a campaign that the NYPD decided to halt funding for, but many of the rank-and-file officers, detectives and district captains never forgave Barron after a fellow officer was killed while Barron was working deep undercover as a drug kingpin trying to buy his way into Queens' music scene.

Weeks later, Barron was on his way to Philly with a half-hearted recommendation from his now-former NYPD captain.

Feeling disrespected, Barron took a deep breath as he spoke, a technique learned that better allowed him to talk to people he was utterly disgusted by without letting them know it.

"Cammie, I don't know much right now, but I do know that I do not know who this individual is," Barron said, now turning an intense, yet sideways, glare to the still-silent man in the other chair.

Barron could tell from his look - dark navy suit, matching tie and bald head - that, whomever he was, he was official and here on official business. "And I don't know about discussing this situation in the presence of anyone not associated with this case."

Barron knew this was going to be a lost argument when the captain leaned forward and planted his meaty palms on his desk, his usually red face illuminated to an even deeper shade of fiery crimson.

"It's none of your goddamned business who is in my office," Cammie boomed. "For far too long you have been given a pass around here, while your superior - me - and MY superiors at the Roundhouse, looked the other way. But that stops here. Tell me what you know about Streaks. Now."

Barron was caught off-guard by Cammie's blast, causing him to writhe just a bit more in his seat.

Stealing a glance to his left, Wilkinson spotted the man, who had no ID badge on, looking dead at him, emotionless.

The detective finally exhaled. This was going to be one long conversation.

"Streaks was an informant. Not unlike the many I dealt with while up in New York and now here in Philly. He was just another street urchin willing to flip on his competition to keep his ass out of a sling. I used him for few shootings in North Philly, plus that sting in Kensington.

"Why he ended up dead or who killed him is beyond me, but I'm sure Streaks had no shortage of enemies himself. The streets are probably talking about it right now."

Barron didn't feel right casting Streaks in an even more of unfavorable light in front of his boss and the stranger, but he also knew that it was in his own best and immediate interest if he seemed as detached from Streaks as possible.

And besides, Barron internally compromised, Streaks was everything the detective said he was.

47

Maybe even more. At any rate, Barron knew his relationship with Streaks didn't have anything at all to do with the rapper getting whacked.

"You are some piece of work, Wilkinson. You came in here on a half-assed recommendation, and all you have to show for it is that shiny suit you're wearing, that fancy car you're driving, a few mid-level stings and now a dead stoolie in your wheelhouse," Cammie said while standing directly in front of Barron, glaring down at his still-seated detective. "And you must think I just docked off the boat from Leinster and hungry for some fuckin' potato soup if you're trying to feed this bullshit to me.

"Everyone around here knows that Streaks was your prime stoolie, and now he's dead. What's worse, this happened in my district, and when you came in here, you promised to bring order to the niggers killing themselves in clubs."

Wilkinson stiffened, and looked through his captain.

"I'll find out who killed Streaks, Cammie. Is that all?" Wilkinson was nearly on his feet as he spoke, rising out of his chair.

"Just one more thing, rap cop. You've got a week to find the killer. The police commissioner is looking to cut department fat by trimming unproductive units. Guess who's unit he's looking at first?

Chapter Four

RANDALL was just stirring in Ivey's arms at about the same time that Barron exited the Cammie grilling.

Randall slid out of bed, went to the bathroom and stared at himself in the mirror.

It seemed that Randall recognized the person looking back at him less and less, and even found himself recently wondering exactly who that individual was staring back at him.

Randall tilted his head, amazed that the image tilted its head in like fashion; Randall then moved his head to the other side, once again lost in wonder at the image's perfect imitation of his moves.

"What the fuck are you looking at?" Randall murmured to the image that just a millisecond ago had cursed him. Randall them moved his face to within an inch of the mirror, to get up close and personal with this lookalike who was talking way too much shit for Randall's liking.

Being an only child, Randall often took to talking to himself, especially in mirrors. The way the image mimicked his every move and said the exact same things as he did always amazed Randall. Over time, the image in the sliver of flat, reflective glass became the sibling Randall never had.

It wasn't long before Randall started speaking to the image in the mirror, and he even believed the image answered him a few times. Those brief encounters have become, especially lately, full bloom conversations.

Way before Ivey, Randall found a profound sense of camaraderie with that singular, lifelong image that was always there when Randall needed him.

Especially in Randall's early teen years.

Back then, Randall had few friends, and those that he did have would always ridicule Randall for one reason or the other. Most of the teasing was due to the fact that he and his mother were dirt poor, growing up first on the city's outside before his mother migrated the family to West Philadelphia.

But the real brunt of the teasing was the truly nerve-wrecking torture at the hands of children in and around the neighborhood who viewed Randall as a different, weird kid. Randall lost count of the fights he got into or the number of times he was jumped. Those experiences lead Randall to build both an established knuckle game and a deep sense of suspicion for new people and surroundings.

Still, Randall was always more of a pacifist than a pugilist; and coupled with a slender build and hesitance to initiate fights or join in a jumping, Randall regularly ended up having all sorts of issues at a time in his life when he still didn't understand much about his own existence.

Randall, almost bringing his eyeball to touch the bathroom mirror, was shaken from his tête-à-tête by Ivey's sexy playfulness.

"Good morning baby. Why you so up on the mirror?" said Ivey, wearing high-cut panties and midriff-bearing t-shirt, as she hugged Randall at the waist. "You don't have to preserve your sexy baby, it's already gone."

Ivey then playfully slapped Randall on the ass before running back into the bedroom, with Randall following.

Once back in bed, Ivey switched on the Sunday morning news, which, along with all the other pre-Eagles football game hype, ran a brief on Streaks murder.

Channel 10's newscast did a live shot from outside Jeronimo's, which didn't even have police tape cordoning of the crime scene anymore. *Figures*, Randall thought, condescendingly. *It was nothing.*

The TV spot again reminded Randall of his looming task once he arrived at the newsroom later that afternoon.

"I'm not looking forward to covering this shit," Randall said before switching the channel to SportsCenter Classic. "He got murked out pretty bad, but you can't tell me Streaks didn't have it coming. Remember that shit with those guns a while back? Streaks never gave a fuck about anyone."

Ivey nodded her head, knowing that Streaks was indeed a calculating person who fully embraced drug hustling and thug rapping; for Streaks, the only code was survival at all cost.

"Indeed. But baby, somewhere in that cold heart of yours, you have to feel sad, at least for the way Streaks went out. You covered enough messy murders to know what it's like," Ivey said while reaching beyond Randall to light the unfinished dutch, left over from a few hours prior. "I still think that shit was pretty hardcore."

Randall pondered Ivey's sentiment while SportsCenter ran a replay of the Phillies' clinching out to win the 2008 World Series.

She had a point. Randall often told her disheartening, somber tales of what murder scenes looked and smelled like.

Randall did enough talking with grieving widows, sons, daughters and friends-of-victims to know what it's like dealing with a murdered love one. Randall will never forget talking to the mother of a slain 14-year-old boy who was shot in the back of the head, at point-bank range, all over $10 bet.

But Randall also knew murders in the 'hood generally cut both ways, as he also covered many an incident of a drug dealer or ice-hearted thug being mowed down by someone even more callous than he.

Those stories didn't feature much grieving; because generally, there weren't many folks around to say how much of a good guy the deceased was. And if there were, they would only provide that usual "died too soon" carp that Randall was all too familiar with.

And that's the category that Randall believed Streaks' belonged in.

Randall, for what it's worth, also kept an ear close enough to the street, and word had it that Streaks' roamed so free because he must have struck some sort of deal with 5-0.

Of course, Randall couldn't prove it, and besides, it wasn't his job to uncover sleazy deals between shady street cats and even shadier police. That was for the paper's cops-and-capers reporting team.

"I guess you're right. It's the reporter in me looking at it objectively," Randall said. "But you've heard how many times Streaks' said he'd kill in his lyrics. I'm just saying, if he lived by that, then maybe he died by that."

Ivey rolled her eyes and elbowed Randall before passing him the blunt. This was turning in to one of those conversations that could get pretty philosophical in a hurry, but Randall knew it would have to be an abbreviated one, as he was due in the newsroom in two hours.

Getting dressed after showering, Randall remembered the high stakes battle between Leviticus IX and Bombay, scheduled for Monday evening at Sidewalk Soco's. Ivey couldn't attend because she would be recording her weekly podcast for Technics, but Randall knew he had to cover that event.

First things first, and that was the assuredly messy work of following up on the murder of Streaks.

"Hey baby, who do you think will win tomorrow's battle?" Ivey said, only partially reading Randall's mind. This was going to be the premier battle so far between two rival emcees, a clash that generated a lot of attention throughout the local hip-hop circuit.

Like everyone else, Ivey often asked Randall his take on the current state of hip-hop; the only difference being that she was genuinely asking and not looking for some sort of angle, like most of the other inquisitors.

It got so bad that folks in the underground would ask her outright to quiz Randall, just to gleam any sort of insider's edge.

Randall never played up the fact that his columns, articles, reviews and write-ups carried considerable weight on the local rap scene, sort of like the written equivalent to Ivey's "Iviest Playlist," which every rapper in Philly wants to be featured on.

Ivey, being Randall's stand-up woman, never passed those questions along to Randall. It's not as if whatever Randall said or thought about a particular emcee or a particular battle was worth noting; but some treated Randall's insight with the sort of venerability usually reserved for a Las Vegas betting line.

"I don't really know. Bombay and Leviticus IX both rhyme about the same shit but have unique styles. When it comes to battle rhyming though, Bombay can be pretty tough to handle with his vicious punch lines, and he can say some really mean-spirited shit," Randall offered in his usual way. "Ten stacks is a hefty chunk of change they're battling for, so I expect this to get personal in a hurry. If it comes down to sheer lyricism, Levi might squeeze out a close victory."

It seemed as though the stakes were raised after each battle, and not just monetarily; Bombay, emboldened by each passing victory, became more audacious, recently appearing on a local hip-hop broadcast and disrespecting Levi's girlfriend and two children. It was something of a Muhammad Ali routine that went entirely too far.

"Anyway baby, it's time for me to get to the newsroom. I'm not looking forward to covering this Streaks' shit, but I am definitely looking forward to getting back to you."

"Okay sweetie," Ivey responded. "Hit me up when you're done, and I'll make sure I'm ready for you."

Sunday and Monday were strict off-the-tables days for Ivey, as Sunday night was throwback disco night at Decibel, and the club was closed on Monday. Ivey would usually spend Saturday night through Monday morning at Randall's apartment, or Randall would spend that time at Ivey's spot.

After Randall made the drive to the paper's main newsroom, which was situated about five miles from Ivey's complex, he called police public affairs, the homicide unit and the medical examiner's office to get the details on Streaks' murder, which were even more gruesome than Randall first thought.

"We got a call for a job at 11:10 Saturday night about a possible homicide in a club on North Indiana Street. The decedent was strangled," said Captain Denise Jones, the usual on-call weekend police supervisor for Police Public Affairs.

She spoke with the careless, faraway monotone of a veteran officer accustomed to giving out murder details on a daily, if not hourly, basis.

Randall and Denise got to know each other through Randall's numerous inquiries and his fair write-ups on police-involved shootings over the years.

"The victim, a 27-year-old black male, was pronounced dead at the scene. We have no motives or suspects."

It was police policy to not reveal the identity of a murder victim until the family has been officially notified, but by Sunday afternoon, everyone knew it was Streaks.

The supervisor also confirmed what Randall already figured: Jeronimo's had no working surveillance system and the security guards were oblivious and otherwise didn't want to get involved. Apparently, there weren't any helpful witnesses to the murder either.

Randall pondered that as he dialed the ME's office to get the official cause of death.

Everyone is on-call on Sundays, Randall muttered to himself, despising the fact that he had to work on Sundays when just about every citywide governmental office was closed.

The weekend ME clerk, after receiving clearance from the weekend director, ran down Streaks' injuries and manner of death in the most sterile and matter-of-fact way imaginable.

"The victim suffered from a severe detachment of the auricular and posterior veins in his neck, and had extreme trauma to his cerebrum," the clerk said, as if reading from a checklist.

"He also suffered major blood loss due to a ruptured internal carotid artery, and a nearly detached brainstem.

Randall wondered what all that meant.

"He was apparently strangled with a very sharp metal of some sort, which only further exacerbated the victim's injuries," the clerk continued. "The trauma suffered to the neck and jaw and also means his skull was violently shaken before dying."

Randall asked if the chain was the only method used in the murder.

"You will have to talk to the examiner about that, but his receiving report does indicate the amount of damage inflicted couldn't have resulted from just a necklace alone, no matter how sturdy the metal," The clerk said. "From what I can conclude, it looks like the killer could have first grabbed the victim from behind by the neck, chocking him through continual, crushing pressure applied by the humerus and radius bone. The introduction of the necklace came after.

"Again, you'll have to speak to the Examiner for any official cause of death and probable methodology."

Randall thanked the clerk and hung up, and felt an odd, lukewarm sensation overtake him. Not a free-of-feeling numbness, but absent were Randall's feelings of depression and introspection that usually directly followed calls like this; in its place was a void of emotion.

In fact, Randall didn't feel much of anything at all about the details of Streaks' murder; for some reason, Randall thought it odd that the clerk referred to Streaks as a victim.

Just then Randall's editor walked over, no doubt wanting a run down.

"It was the usual fare from public affairs and the ME's office," Randall said, without turning to face Sue McCombs, another of the paper's weekend news editors. "As per the norm, our friends over at homicide said they wouldn't have anything substantial for the press until tomorrow, but to not expect a press conference over it. I'm going to head out to Jeronimo's, just to check out the scene. I'll file maybe 16 inches or so when I get back."

Editors like Sue loved leaving the 'hood shit to Randall, especially matters that involved the local rap scene mixed with murder. In a strange way, that is what Randall was there for, after all.

At that moment, several miles away, Detective Barron Wilkinson, having squeezed one of the security guards for a key, was now squinting through the dark haze that had enveloped Jeronimo's interior ever since it closed after Streaks was murdered.

Inside the squalor club, Barron took care to look at every minute detail as he went from the bar, to the stage, back to the bar, through both bathrooms and the soundroom, hoping to find any clue that would lead to Streaks' killer.

As he searched, Barron thought of the many enemies Streaks must have amassed over the years, including a few very vocal ones who bought into the theory of Streaks being a 'hood snitch.

Barron thought of the escalating murder rate and shook his head. *Everyone in this filthy town is a killer.*

No matter who did it, Barron thought, it wasn't by accident. Whoever did this meant to do it and left a macabre parting message as well.

It was probably some pissed off rival rapper, Barron surmised, as he stepped through sticky puddles of a congealing mix of beer and regurgitated beer to make his way to the greenroom. *But whoever offed Streaks must've been pretty strong to jump him.*

90 minutes into his so-far futile search, Barron stumbled upon a clue that he hoped would put him on the path to Streaks killer.

Kneeling, the detective took a small evidence packet from his pocket, and with the included forceps, he picked up a piece of Streaks' shredded platinum chain which was caught between an upended chair and a drab curtain partition. Barron hoped forensics could work the shard over and maybe come up with at least a partial fingerprint.

Amazed that the crime scene team missed it, Barron analyzed the piece of jewelry, turning it over and over, its edges catching the dim light and causing an eerie, crimson-tinged spotlight to bounce from the link and reflect on the nearest wall.

After securing the link inside the cellophane bag, the detective picked up the chair that was apparently upended in the struggle and surveyed the scene, positioning himself on the couch as Streaks most likely would have moments before his killer claimed his life.

*****

RANDALL could think of a number of things he would rather be doing instead of heading back over to Jeronimo's, but this was for business, Randall thought, and besides, the club would be closed, and no one would be around who would willingly talk about what happened. Still, he had to make a go of it.

Parking a few spaces behind a nondescript but very official looking Chrysler with tinted windows, Randall wondered which detectives were wasting their Sunday afternoon by talking to uncooperative neighbors.

In the afternoon sun, Indiana Avenue almost looked serene, mocking the murder that occurred just hours prior.

After taking in the exterior and jotting down a few notes, Randall instinctively pulled on the front door to the club.

Randall's senses jolted with alarm as he found the door unlocked.

Stepping inside, the raw, unmistakable funk of the dank hip-hop club filled Randall's nostrils, almost making him cough. After rubbing his eyes, Randall saw a tall figure emerge from the darkened stairwell at the far end of the club.

"Who are you and what are you doing here?" Barron said. His gruff tone and the fact that his inquisitor was alone gave Randall reason for pause.

"My name is Randall Jenkins, and I am a reporter with the Philly Times," Randall retorted while reaching for his ever-faithful Press Pass and ID. "I'm here doing a story on the murdered rapper."

Barron slowed his gait as he approached Randall. "I've read some of your pieces. That thing you did on West Philly gentrification was clever, but you've missed the true angles in a number of your crime stories."

Over the years, Randall has developed a very thick skin and had grown accustomed to people second-guessing and critiquing his work, but he often at least knew from where or from whom the criticism was coming.

"Something my editors tell me all the time," Randall said. "But who are you?"

Now stepping into full view and the light from the splintered rays of sunlight beaming into the club through a fractured window, Randall could now see who he was talking to, but couldn't quite place the face. He knew for certain that it wasn't one of the usual weekend homicide detectives.

"My name is Detective Barron Wilkinson, and I'm here doing the same as you, looking for clues," Barron said, extended his hand. "Maybe we could exchange notes."

Randall always relished the opportunity to share field notes with an on-scene detective. Rarely does it happen, but when it does, Randall usually would reap a bounty of insider information that no other reporter could acquire.

"Well, I don't know much. Streaks, like everyone else, had his friends and he had his enemies," Randall said after shaking Barron's hand. "Of his enemies, there's no one I can think of that would have the balls to wack him, especially on a night that he's performing. It just doesn't make sense."

Barron nodded.

"And the fact that he had his whole crew here, and that everyone knew everybody else that was there, just makes his killing even more bizarre."

Randall waited for Barron to reciprocate. The seconds thumped by like minutes, as Randall stood in silence.

Randall was prepared for the one-sided exchange to end right there.

"Well?"

"I want to know what you think about the reputation Streaks had about being a pigeon," Barron said, and for the first time looked Randall fully in the eyes. "I know you hear a lot of things. Have you heard that?"

Struck by the question and not at all appreciative of Detective Barron Wilkinson's tone and approach, Randall shot back a deft answer.

"I don't particularly care about his supposed dealings with your bosses," Randall said sharply. "Sure, I have heard that Streaks was on someone's payroll, but unless I witnessed any sort of payoff or overheard or was present for any incriminating conversations, that's all speculation and hearsay. I leave that to the cloak-and-dagger investigative reporters who enjoy a much higher pay grade than mine.

"Frankly, it's none of my business, and since it isn't, I like to remain healthy; being a reporter doesn't make me bulletproof, you know.

So, what can you share about Streaks?"

Barron sighed and sat on a tattered barstool.

"Look here, Randall. What I am going to tell you is official police information. As top-level as it is, I actually feel confident telling you, precisely because you are the only person in the media who will know this as fact."

Barron looked at Randall with a long, hard stare to make sure the veiled threat got through. *In other words,* Randall thought silently, *I'm in for a shitstorm of drama if I let this out. Gotcha.*

It's great that Randall was getting the scoop. Not so great is that he couldn't share it, and even less great was the fact that Randall would be the only one on the other side of the thin blue line to know.

But Randall always believed in his newspaperman ethics, so this wasn't too much of a problem. Not yet, at least.

Looking around as if someone was there who clearly wasn't, Barron spoke so low Randall could barely hear him. As if they were sharing granddad's brandy, Randall got in close.

"Streaks was semi-officially on the police payroll, but he wasn't the level of snitch that the streets perceived him to be," Barron said. "While he did flip on a few of his competitors who were likewise wanted by the department, Streaks' true value to the department was not in the telling, but in the doing."

"Doing of what?" Randall blurted out in a loud whisper. Now all in, Randall wanted to know, once and for all, what the fuck Streaks was in to, and how he, up until Saturday night, managed to roam so free for so long.

Rolling his eyes at Randall's eagerness, Barron explained.

"Who you've only known as Streaks is really Reginald Strong, and he was into drug selling long before he ever got into rapping, and not the other way around. In fact, one could say that his drug dealing got him into rapping. You also may know a little something about his gun charges that were dropped."

Oh shit, Randall thought, while remaining silent. *This is going to be an all-time scoop.*

"See, at the time when Reginald caught that gun charge, he was already working for the department as a confidential informant. Reginald, like most street criminals without a long-term plan, was caught selling weed around 29th and Hunting Park. Not too much of an offense in and of itself, but the real problem for Reginald was the 15 grams of crack cocaine he also had on him; it wasn't much about the gun, as everyone, you included, probably assumed. That gun would only be used as a prop later to bring him in when he became…reluctant to talk to us.

"Reginald was desperate not to go back to jail and vowed to do anything, including flip on his closest friends, to not be forcibly booked for a multi-year stay at one of the state-run hotels out in the sticks, far away from everything and everyone he held dear. So, he gave us a few names and locations, and Reginald was able to go free while we busted a heroin ring in Kensington.

"But instead of just paying Reginald, the department thought it would be an excellent idea to fund his lifestyle, make him bigger than life itself, so that he could lead the department to bigger and more important figures in the drug game. Thus, the persona known as 'Streaks' was really born."

Randall noted just a tinge of regret in Barron's retelling.

Barron then pulled out a pack of Newports, drew one, lit it and took a long puff before continuing.

"But Reginald, now known far and wide as Streaks, allowed the persona that we, well, the department created, to go to his head and he began skipping his weekly check-ins with us, going on for about three months at the time of his slaying. This is now the second time Streaks purposely fell of our radar; the first time Streaks forgot what he owed the department, we brought him in, straight off the streets."

"How?" Randall asked.

"Informing goes both ways. Streaks wasn't the only birdie I had out there, and a few of them chirped on Streaks," Barron Said. "We had it on good information that Streaks always carried a certain Dessert Eagle, because we gave it to him," Barron said in a revelation that almost made Randall's ears drop out of his ass. "So it wasn't that hard for a traffic sting unit to pull him over for a bullshit traffic offense, pat him down, search the vehicle and find the gun and drugs. We didn't give him the smack though, and that posed a problem for the whole operation.

"We brought Streaks in to remind him of his debt to the department and to make him understand that just as easily as we made his $90,000 truck, his jewelry and his around-the-way fame happen, we can snatch it all away just as fast if he didn't cooperate.

"That was the deal he agreed to."

Barron wiped sweat beads from his brow and took another puff of his short before continuing.

"Even though Reginald failed to see what he owed to the department, he was wise enough to also know that he couldn't risk his cover being blown. By that time, he began to really embody his lyrics and he embellished his lifestyle even more, and we became certain that Reginald believed what he was saying about killing snitches and being untouchable, all the while he was the biggest snitch the streets have seen in quite some time."

Some of that made sense. But just then, Randall had a burning question.

"But what about Streaks' crew? Why didn't they intervene last night, and where are they now?"

Barron shrugged.

"Who fuckin' knows? We do know that while they all may have been homeboys, none of them would take a bullet for him, and we didn't attempt to flip anyone in his crew. And besides, we confirmed their whereabouts during the time of the murder; they were all there at the club. Otherwise, they aren't saying much, and we don't expect much cooperation from them, anyway

As he paused the retelling, Barron again reached for his Newports and this time drew two, lit both and passed the other to Randall.

Randall wasn't a cigarette smoker, but he took Barron's unsaid peace offering and, using the officer's lighter, lit it.

Randall and Barron sat in silence for a few minutes with each puffing on cigarettes in a contemplative manner.

Randall was still digesting this news, which basically confirmed much of what he already figured, but before he could ask a follow-up, Barron's stream of consciousness continued.

"I mean, how do you think he could afford the clothes? The bling? The car? There's not enough underground in the world to support such a lavish lifestyle, not even in a market as big as Philly's. Trust me, I know," Barron said. "Think about it; has Streaks ever been on national radio, or even regional? If you think hard enough, it's not too hard to conclude that Streaks' lifestyle was all just a front, driven by something else."

It was true that Streaks didn't have a proper album out, and that he hasn't made any cameos on albums by other national artists. He had a few singles and mixtapes on streaming services and performed locally, but that was about it.

And the national acts that made it out of Philly didn't mention his name. It was as if Streaks really didn't exist, save for a few people within a few square miles knowing who he was.

Still, Randall wanted to know what all this had to do with Streaks being murdered, and why the detective was telling him all of this official information.

"So why didn't the department just cut ties with Streaks?" Randall asked. "It seems like you could have pulled the rug from under him at any given time."

"We decided to give him just a bit more rope and leeway," Barron said. "I was to reconnect with him, but as you can see, his death interceded my catching up with him."

Detective Barron Wilkinson decided it best not to tell anyone, especially a reporter, that he was going to meet Streaks on the very night the rapper was killed.

"Wow. Appreciative as I am, why are you telling me all this?" Randall asked. "You know that I can't do anything with it. Are you trying to trap me up or something? I've been around the block, and I have had my articles called into evidence one too many times for my liking."

"Oh, I am sure you will know what to do when the time comes," Barron said, standing to leave and motioning for Randall to stand as well, as the detective would surely reseal the scene after their departure. "I trust you'll know the right thing to do."

Randall's senses were buzzing when he left the club and returned to the newsroom. On the way, he telephoned his editor with the details of his trip, omitting his one-on-one with Barron. It ended up being the usual follow up to a rather mundane crime assignment.

"That's great," Sue said. "Come back and file 15 inches for Monday's paper."

*****

A PROMISE to Detective Barron Wilkinson was one thing, but Randall couldn't wait to catch up to Ivey to let her know about their chat. If there was one person on the planet that Randall could entrust with confidential information, it was Ivey.

What was newsworthy or a shocking revelation to Randall hardly registered with Ivey; not that she didn't care, but Ivey chalked it all up as part of the newspaper game, something of which she had no interest in, given the types of stories that Randall worked on. And Randall often brought enough emotional baggage home from work to break both of their backs. She long ago decided to never add to that.

After filing his article, Randall made it back to Ivey's apartment where she was waiting for him.

"So how was work, baby? Any news?" Ivey always asked that question with a bright smile, like it was a good-natured pun.

"Well, your boy Streaks was a snitch, I hate to say; maybe his posthumous release will be titled 'Hood Dimes.'" Randall said, before peeling out of his clothes.

Ivey sat up before tapping out the ashes of the spliff she was enjoying prior to Randall's arrival.

"You're one cold-blooded brother," Ivey said. "But shit, everyone thought he was a snitch, though. What's so new about that?" Randall thought for a long second, pondering whether or not to inform his soulmate directly of his clandestine meeting with the detective.

"Well, I got it on good info that Streaks was getting that department dough; a string of payouts and a shitload of front money," Randall said, while running down his chance encounter with Detective Barron Wilkinson. "See, I knew it all along; Streaks was going to get what was coming. It's a shame, though, but maybe someone finally had enough of his frontin' ass and did him in." Ivey threw a pillow at Randall before passing him a fresh spliff and a lighter. "Here, Mr. Frosty, maybe this will help you warm up."

Chapter Five

MONDAY arrived entirely too early for Randall. One of the main downfalls about working the Sunday late afternoon and Monday morning swing shift was being out of sorts when it came to reporting for duty on Monday mornings. Still, Randall had a job to do, so he slipped out of bed, showered and left a still-dozing Ivey and headed for the newsroom.

Usually one the first reporters to arrive on Mondays, Randall was a bit surprised to see the dayside editor there, who promptly quizzed Randall on the killing over the weekend.

"Do you really think it had anything to do with his music?" asked Gretchen McAllister, in her usually sincere way. Gretchen, when inquiring about a taboo or sensitive topic, was always one to ask in the most sensitive way possible, and Randall respected her for that. "I think it all revolves around his violent lifestyle."

"You're probably right," Randall replied, forcing out at bit of sentimentality for Streaks' demise. "I filed all I had on it. If nothing else develops outside of what the police and witnesses can provide, then I think that will be all there is to the story of the murdered Streaks."

Randall hated lying to Gretchen, because he knew there was much, much more to the story. But he also wanted to hedge his bets with Detective Barron Wilkinson; something just wasn't right with him, and until Randall could figure out Barron's angle, he wasn't about to poke around the case, nor let his editors know of his connection.

"I see you're on the budget for that hip-hop show tonight; you're working hard," Gretchen said. "We assigned photo for it. Looks like you should be good for about 20 inches. Since you've already filed and are working tonight, you can skip on out after you e-mail me your budgetline. Hopefully there's no shootings at that thing, right?"

Monday's night's event felt like a Pay-Per-View showdown; digital turntable producer MixedMikes and electronics outfit B&B Outlets sponsored this event, including putting up the $10,000 purse. There was even gold "Rapper Heavyweight Title" belt that would go to the winner.

Randall had long ago stopped participating as a judge in these events, do to hostile and salty emcees who would physically threaten for voting against certain performers. It got so bad that Randall thought long and hard about getting a gun to brace himself when out and about.

Eventually, Randall thought better of the idea of getting a hammer, if for no other reason than it wouldn't be a good look for a well-known writer to get caught out there with a piece.

Although the battle was scheduled for much later in the evening at Sidewalk Soco's, a trendy club in Brewerytown, Randall was allowed to leave the newsroom on his own time due to the after-hours nature of his assignment; but Randall appreciated the official green-light from Gretchen just the same.

Before leaving, Randall noticed that the paper's top crime and police reporting team had checked in for their usual shift of chasing blood trails and bullet casings. Right then, Randall decided to see if he could gleam any info on the background of Detective Barron Wilkinson.

"Hey Stickie, I have a question for you. I met this detective yesterday, Barron Wilkinson, new to the department. You know anything about him?"

Meg "Stickie" Patterson and Alex Mahorn made up the paper's ace crime-writing duo, and Stickie made it a point to get to know every detective in the department - especially new ones she could sink her claws in to.

"Hey Randall. Good shit on that rapper murder, but I wish weekend photo was assigned. They never get it right, always missing the blood and ambulance. Anyway, I don't know much about Wilkinson, but I do know he came here from New York," Stickie said, while shuffling through the news releases of fresh departmental hires and her own notes. "Here it is. Yeah, Detective Barron Wilkinson…hired on recommendation…led to successful prosecution of various music-based crime rings…involved in a high-profile rap-related bust in Queens."

Randall had a sickening feeling that he now knew exactly who Detective Barron Wilkinson was. Randall groaned. *Fuck me.*

"Thanks, Stickie. I owe you one."

"Yeah, yeah," Stickie said. "You've owed me a drink ever since that Camansky piece."

*****

WHILE leaving the newsroom, thoughts of the murdered Streaks and the upcoming battle were sidetracked by the fresh information provided by Stickie. Randall cursed himself as he didn't recognize the infamous Detective Barron Wilkinson when he first heard the name.

Randall heard of the notorious and heretofore anonymous "Hip-Hop Cop" well before his journalism career took off in earnest.

Often dismissed as tinfoil chatter amongst the backpacker and hustler types, there were rumors of a cop in New York who looked and acted the part of a monied music mogul, only to betray his connections which led to many of them being sent to Rikers Island. The rumors grew teeth when a few of them were released and began telling everyone about this dingy cop.

Walking to his car, Randall recalled hearsay of a particularly bad episode in Queens. The story went that an undercover detective showed up on the scene posing as well-heeled producer from Atlanta that was looking to set up shop in the borough.

NYPD made sure the rouse would work, even going so far as to set up a fake office front and creating a false call-through for the phantom operation in Atlanta.

The front was enough to convince many street rappers to gravitate toward Barron, but not everyone bought the detective's propped-up visage.

Franc Politik, one of the rappers that Barron pinched in Queens and who was later released because the evidence against him was rather flimsy, made it his business to tell everyone who would listen that not only was Barron an undercover cop, but that the detective also should be shot dead upon sight by any of the street gangs running in the city. He even told those very real shooters what Barron looked like, along with his mannerisms.

Two weeks after that, Franc was found dead in his Jackson Heights apartment.

Randall wasn't sure of all the details, but it also had something to do with some guns and drugs being found in the apartment as well.

Randall thought this was bad; but then, an odd feeling surged through his veins; a mix of exciting encouragement and a spiked sense of curiosity.

Randall often felt this way when he was genuinely intrigued by a battle of wits. As he slid into his Honda, Randall again thought of the detective and when - and how - the two would next engage.

Randall knew that no one ever volunteered information free of charge. Especially high-ranking detectives. Through his dealings with all sorts of cretins both in uniform and in civilian attire, Randall knew that information always came with a price.

That price could be that someone is trying to burn a third party by leaking out details to the press; it could also be that the reporter is being fed information that is incorrect by design, which would be used as some sort of smokescreen effort conducted by the effected party; sort of a disinformation campaign.

As a reporter, Randall has seen it all, and then seen some more.

It was telling that the media, by and large, moved on from Streaks' murder, and by late Monday afternoon, it was an afterthought in the underground as well, as attention turned to the battle to come.

See, no one gave a fuck about Streaks, Randall mused to himself as he crossed the street to make his way to the newsroom garage. *Not even his own crew. Guess, in the end, he got what he deserved.*

Just then, Randall's cell vibrated with "DJIV" on the caller ID.

"What's good, baby? I'm just leaving the newsroom now."

"It's all good, love." Ivey's melodic voice poured from Randall's phone like sweet tea, sending a cool vibe through him. "I wanted to know if we could catch up before the battle tonight, if you're free…"

"Of course, sweetness. I'm on my way to you now," Randall said, instantly forgetting about his own plans to prep for the battle at his place. But since he always kept sets of fresh clothes at Ivey's apartment, relaxing with her before the show was probably the better plan.

Just then, Randall had a thought. He knew Ivey was plugged in, in her own special way, to the bigger news of the rap world, and she would at times know about a situation even before Randall did. Ivey also was a master hobbyist of connecting the dots. Randall always thought that had something to do with Ivey minoring in Statistics while at Drexel.

"Hey baby, remember that new cop, the one from New York that I told you about, Detective Barron Wilkinson? I just have a strange feeling about dude, like he knows more about the scene than he lets on," Randall said. "And Stickie said he was involved in some anti-rap task force there. Can you ask around real quick with your New York connects, see if they know anything about him?"

Randall hated asking Ivey to do things like this, but he just couldn't shake his theory.

"Okay baby, I'll make some calls and talk to a few people. Now you just get over here to me."

The paper's garage, located directly behind the building and just beyond the loading docks, was an altogether dark and dreary place, contrasting the many glass-skinned buildings and twinkling skyscrapers of its neighbors.

Randall, though, never felt a sense of apprehension using the garage, until now. Something didn't feel right when Randall entered, and he felt creeped out by a noise in the distance.

I must be out of my fuckin' mind, Randall thought, glancing past the off-limits row of executive slots filled with the Mercedes Benz and Aston Martin owned by the publisher and editor-in-chief, respectively. *I need to get some sleep.*

Randall climbed the steps to the second floor of the garage to his parked Accord. Just as Randall thought it was darker than usual in the garage, he noticed a silhouetted figure walking up the stairwell at the other end.

Probably just security, Randall mused. Pulling out his keys, he chirped his Accord.

"What's good, homeboy?" The voice startled Randall, causing him to drop his keys. "I heard you're going to write about tonight's battle."

Marcus' presence in the secured parking lot confounded Randall, but he tried to mask any show of surprise.

"Yeah, you know, I usually cover the underground scene. How did you get in here?" Randall asked.

"The guard downstairs let me up when I said I was a friend of yours. I really wanted to catch up to you and ask about Streaks, though. Did the police say anything?"

Randall was put off by the question, because he was already asked a million times by a million different people.

"Nope, nothing new from the cops. No motives, no witness, no one caring; nothing."

Marcus smiled before letting out full-bellied laugh, as if he just heard the greatest joke ever told. But just as quickly as his smile and laughter appeared, it was gone. "I told you he wouldn't cause you any problems."

"But I never had any real problem with Streaks," Randall said, instinctively defensive. "He would do his thing and I would do mine, and that was that."

With that, Randall retrieved his dropped keys, got into his Honda and turned the engine on. Marcus cocked his head from right to left as he stepped aside to allow Randall to back out his Accord. Randall wished he didn't ask, but...

"I'm heading out to see Ivey. Which reminds me. How do you know her?"

For the first time in their acquaintance, Randall really focused in on Marcus, buffeting his serious tone with a just-as-serious facial expression.

Marcus again laughed out loud, his voice echoing off the garage walls.

"So what time are you going to the battle?" Marcus asked, completely ignoring Randall's question. "I figured we could link up, swing through together."

For some reason, Randall just didn't feel like hanging out with Marcus, but couldn't quite blow him off.

"Well, when I'm on official business, like tonight, I usually roll through about 30 minutes before the first set. The paper assigned a photographer to go with me tonight, so I'll have to play it pretty much straight up."

Marcus frowned lasted for a split-second, replaced by a big, toothy grin.

"Ahh, the paper doing it up big for my mans," Marcus said, his voice ricocheting off the inner walls of Randall's cranium. "I'm sure there will be something worth catching on film."

Marcus calmly walked off, disappearing as quickly as he emerged through the low-lying haze that enveloped the second floor of the garage. Mystified and confused by Marcus' behavior, Randall shifted his car, reversed out of his spot, and left.

Randall felt as though the haze from the garage somehow mixed with his brain's gray matter, as he was unable to shake the weird vibes he was catching from Marcus.

A blow of the horn from an impatient driver jolted Randall from his thoughts, and when he finally made it to Ivey's apartment, he had the most startling and amazing thought.

That thought, however, would have to wait, as Ivey greeted him at the door, looking flushed and slightly pale, with a jaundice of worry replacing her usually colorful complexion.

She grabbed Randall by the arm, locked the door behind them both, and without saying a word, dragged him to the bedroom.

"This is what I found on your detective, and you're not going to like it."

Ivey pointed to her MacBook, and on its screen was an article from the New York Gazette.

Randall's eyes grew wider and wider with every sentence he read.

"…Detective Barron Wilkinson, of New York's highly-controversial, so-called 'Hip-Hop Investigative Squad,' has either assisted in or directly arrested several rappers, first by infiltrating their organizations, most often posing as a record label executive, gaining their trust before …"

Randall felt weak as he continued reading.

"Thanks to the work of Wilkinson and others, more than a dozen criminals masquerading as rappers have been arrested and found guilty of numerous crimes, including murder-for-hire plots and money laundering."

The article went on to read that the department's operations had been shut down due to some illegality and complaints from watchdog groups and neighborhood police advisory councils.

"If you think that's bad," Ivey said, "read this next one."

Randall could hardly breathe let alone take a moment to digest what he had just read before Ivey clicked on her keyboard to bring up the other page in her browser.

This article took a much closer look into the details of Detective Barron Wilkinson's role in an illicit and complex drug ring and fencing scheme. The article pointed out the while the detective was never officially charged with anything, the evidence reeked with his involvement.

Randall looked up at Ivey as she took a long, hard pull on a freshly-rolled Backwood that Randall was surely going to need after reading this shit.

"And that's not all, baby. I called a few deejays I know in New York. They all told me that Barron is much worse than a cop. He is a ruthless traitor and bloodthirsty shield who will step on anyone - ANYONE - to get the arrest and his name in the paper," Ivey said. "I also spoke to my copyright lawyer in Brooklyn. Although criminal defense is not his forte, he has given pro-bono advice to several of the rappers Barron crossed up. They all told him that Barron is bad business, and it's not even safe for anyone to be associated with him in business or otherwise, unless you're a cop.

"Word has it that there is a loose hit out on him right now, and you know how those Queens shooters play."

Ivey silently passed Randall the Backwood, giving it a moment for it to sink in.

Randall recomposed himself, finished both articles, and took a deep, full-lunged pull himself before passing the blunt back to Ivey.

"So, what does all this mean? If those rappers were really into something ill and criminal, is it Barron's fault that they were trusting of him? And isn't it better that criminals, rapper or not, are off the streets?" Randall finally said. "It does seem pretty foul that Barron used them then arrested them, though. But everybody uses someone in that game."

Randall didn't bother to mention that bribes, payoffs and bailouts often too contributed to those exact allegiances.

Ivey exhaled a pungent, whitish cloud that only a properly rolled Backwood could create.

"Yeah, but what if he used journalists as well?" Ivey said, as she sat back and looked at Randall with alert, yet bloodshot eyes.

Before Randall could answer, Ivey leaned over, clicked on a third tab in her Firefox browser and brought up her e-mail. "Here, read this."

Randall, Backwood in hand, began reading the highlighted message. The blunt slipped from Randall's fingers as he shook his head in disbelief.

"I don't believe it," Randall said, looking at Ivey as she bent down to pick up the floored blunt. "I just don't believe Barron would do something like that."

"That's because underneath all of your talk about turning a cold heart when you feel you need to, you really are a trusting person," Ivey said, in a low, sad tone. "But you and I both know Dominique, and now we know why she is a 'former' reporter for Video Two. Your boy Barron, whether you want to believe it or not, is a bloodsucker, and he doesn't and won't hesitate to use and discard folks. Even reporters. Even you."

Randall's head was spinning as he began to put the pieces together.

"This is some odd shit. Made even odder by Marcus' little visit today."

"You seen Marcus today?" Ivey asked. "What did he want?"

"Nothing really, just asked about the battle, if I am going, shit like that. But you know, I had the strangest thought about dude."

"What?"

"Well, that maybe he had something to do with Streaks' murder," Randall answered.

Ivey let the Backwood dangle between her lips for a few seconds before passing it back to Randall.

"What would make you think that?" She asked.

"Just how he has been talking about it; how…nonchalant he seemed about the whole thing. It was like it was a big joke and not a problem, as if Streaks never existed," Randall said. "It's a strange feeling; I can't really put my finger on it."

Randall tilted his head back, closed his eyes and took yet another long pull from the rapidly shrinking Backwood. He felt himself slowly losing grip of this situation, and Randall, if anything, had an uncanny knack for having firm grasps on facts.

Facts are what ruled Randall; he often based his arguments and indeed his whole life's philosophy on facts.

"Well baby, looks like you really know how to make new friends. Friends you should steer clear of," Ivey said.

No shit, Randall thought. *I don't think I can handle many more friends like these.*

Ivey and Randall spent a few hours lounging around her apartment as it grew near time for Randall to head to Sidewalk Soco, and for Ivey to get ready to record her weekly podcast.

Ivey was silently turning over in her mind the revelations concerning Barron and her theory that he was bound to use Randall, sooner or later, and that when he does, Randall will be the one to suffer.

But instead of meddling, Ivey refocused on making sure her man's head was straight for his work tonight.

"Baby, how are you feeling? You ready for tonight? You've been through a lot of shit, and the paper is really making you pull double-duty by covering inner-city crime and this hip-hop culture of ours," Ivey said. "Just making sure you're good."

Randall actually thought of calling his editor to say he had second thoughts on the story and wouldn't attend, but he would need a better reason than 'not feeling like it' to call off the story, especially since photo was assigned.

"I feel about as good as I am going to, love; at least I'm not judging," Randall said, as he dressed in his usual nondescript-yet-fly way. "It's a straight-ahead piece. I'm actually surprised the paper wants to cover it."

"I'm not. Why wouldn't they want the best hip-hop reporter in the world to cover a major battle?" Ivey said, as she hugged Randall from the back before putting a freshly rolled spliff to his mouth. "You know you're the nicest."

Turning, Randall ashed the spliff and pecked Ivey. "No baby, you're the nicest. I'm lucky to have you in my corner."

Ivey smiled, tossed Randall his "go" bag filled with his lucky pen, press pass, backup micro digital recorder and a small reporter's notebook, and gave him another hug.

"You be safe tonight, okay?"

At that moment and several miles away, Detective Barron Wilkinson dressed himself up as the average old-head rap fan, save for his gold badge and the Walther PP .45 caliber tucked in under his sweater in the small of his back, and looked himself in the mirror. Randall was going to have company at tonight's battle.

*****

THE battle at Sidewalk Soco brought out the who's-who of Philly's music scene.

Randall walked past several pimped-out trucks and coupes that undoubtedly belonged to the city's movers and shakers. *Damn, I guess there's money in this underground shit after all,* Randall mused to himself in a way that brought a sarcastic grin to the corners of his mouth. *I wonder how much this Yukon cost? Probably four times as much as my little whip.*

Getting closer to Soco's, Randall spotted several cars and trucks owned by various radio and TV stations, all with the telltale full-body screen wraps advertising their station or their particular "hot" artist.

Randall was one to usually wait on line, but since he was on official business tonight, he flashed his press pass and was ushered through the workers' entrance, skipping the usual security pat-down prerequisite.

Once inside, Randall was greeted by several underground and unsigned rappers in attendance, many of whom he interviewed and formed some degree of mutual respect.

Randall settled into a stool at the far end of the bar which was situated near the stage but definitely out of the way, as he wanted to be as inconspicuous as possible.

That was always Randall's way; be there, but not be; see, but not be seen.

Randall never liked too much attention in his adult years, perhaps because he received so little of it in his youth. Part of it too was that as an adult, Randall became a cynical introvert; if he lived without attention for this long, there was no reason to now need it.

DJ Splice was warming the crowd up with his unique blends but slowed things down and lowering the music for a moment of silence for the recently departed Streaks.

"We can't really do this without first paying respects to a fallen comrade," Splice said over the barely audible instrumental of what was to be Streaks next single, "Fila Money."

"Streaks is probably battling God right now for the title of Best Rapper in Heaven," Splice said. "We miss you, big homie."

The entire crowd bowed their heads for the moment of silence, when a split-second later and in unison, the entire crowed raised sparked lighters, bottles and drinks toward the ceiling.

Randall was stunned by the outpouring of misplaced love, and let his eyes wander about the room and noticed members of the now-splintered Gravytrain camp were not joining the crowd in paying respect to their expired leader. The deejay yanked Randall from his quarry.

"Now let's get this party started!" Splice yelled, and the crowd erupted as a clear briefcase filled with hundreds and fifties was brought to the stage by two very big and very mean looking men, each equipped with equally menacing Glocks stuffed in holsters. A third guard trailed the pair, holding the championship belt high above his head.

Splice set the briefcase on one pedestal, and a lone spotlight shined down on it, further illuminating its rich contents; he then sat the belt on the other pedestal.

An organized rhyme battle would usually start after both Bombay and Leviticus IX did individual sets of their own best material, and after it was decided who would go first, the battle would commence; but those formalities were dashed for this showdown, as this main event would skip those performances and go straight to the battle portion.

As Randall waiting for the contest to begin, a familiar gloved hand slid a rum and coke across the deal-topped bar.

The tumbler seemed to slide down to Randall's end of the bar in slow-motion.

"I thought that was you outside," Marcus said, looking Randall dead in the eyes. It seemed that Marcus appeared out of the thin air. "I think Bombay is going to take Levi in this one."

Randall noticed that his blood ran a little colder whenever Marcus was around.

"I don't really care who wins," Randall said, "as long as it's good and there's no drama."

Randall didn't want drama for a number of reasons, the foremost being that if some shit did break out, he would most likely have to cover it for the paper, and that equaled hazard duty, which he felt the paper certainly wasn't paying him for.

Besides, Randall would like for there to just be a clean battle and that's it; for once.

Marcus leaned in close.

"I was thinking about Streaks when I came in," Marcus said. I wanted to warn you about your new homeboy, Barron."

Randall, fighting his instincts, remained silent but could feel his temples throbbing. The kind of throbbing that sounded and felt like a dull, incessant drumroll.

"I know the department put him on the case, and that he was bound to talk to you," Marcus said. "My advice to you is, don't talk to him anymore."

Randall didn't take at all too kindly to sideways threats such as these, and he just about had enough.

It sounded as though Marcus wanted to actually protect Barron somehow; like there was something to hide. In something less than a heartbeat, Randall deduced that Marcus and Barron were somehow connected, and it may be time to treat them as one and the same.

That instantaneous thought process made Randall bristle, as he remembered the last time he received a warning such as this.

Randall, remaining seated, turned his whole body toward Marcus, and studied him.

"Now dig that shit, coming from you. You know my lady but won't tell me how; you show up where I'm at and I don't even know you like that. And now you want to give me advice?" Randall said, his irritation on the verge of exploding.

It wasn't just his seemingly uncanny insight into Randall's thoughts, but for Randall, Marcus seemed to always pop up at the wrong time.

"Don't worry about my safety, fam. I don't know if you know, but I have been a reporter for a very,

very long time, and I know my way around the department. Believe it, I can handle myself. Detective Barron Wilkinson doesn't scare me, even if he is the so-called 'Hip-Hop Cop.' Rest assured, I got this. But thank you, though."

Randall instantly wished he hadn't let that out. Marcus looked at Randall, but it was too late to show any weakness, so Randall maintained his aggressive posture.

"Oh, okay cousin, I see that you've got Barron all figured out," Marcus said, tilting his head to the right and cracking that slim, almost imperceptible smile of his. "Don't say I didn't warn you."

With that, Marcus got up, put a ten-dollar bill on the table, and made his way across the floor to the other side of club, disappearing from Randall's vision.

Randall momentarily regretted the tone of his exchange with Marcus, a fleeting sentiment interrupted by Splice's introduction of the two emcees.

While Bombay, in full party-starter/hype-man mode, paced back and forth on one side of the stage, Leviticus IX nonchalantly stood in the center on the other side of the stage but directly in front of Bombay, casually sipping from a bottle of water.

The bright rack lights hanging from the club's ceiling shone down on the two lyrical pugilists, indeed giving the event that PPV feel.

Bombay, the odds-on favorite to walk away with the cash and the fame, went first. Beforehand, each emcee agreed upon which instrumentals to use, and unlike other battles, they were allowed to pick different beats. Bombay, rhyming over the instrumental to the "Peter Piper" hit by Run D.M.C., went first.

Randall noticed that Bombay didn't have his usual zest and stage presence; also absent was Bombay's usually too-close-to-home punchlines. The crowd was lukewarm to Bombay, and the Leviticus IX noticed.

Levi, seemingly emboldened by Bombay's relatively weak offering, rhymed over the classic instrumental of Audio Two's 'Top Billin'.

In unleashing a brand-new flow, Levi took the battle straight to Bombay, mocking his flow, his gear and his neighborhood. It was quite the one-sided battle.

Randall instantly recognized Levi's technique as the inside-out, multi-line, multi-syllabic rhyme style made famous by Rakim.

That was pretty dope, Randall thought, while jotting down a few notes.

The crowd ate it up.

Levi easily won the first round, and by the time the second round was over, it was evident that a third round would not be necessary. Everyone knew that Bombay had lost this battle.

Everyone except Bombay himself.

After the votes were tallied, Splice raised Levi's hand right before the two money handlers handed Levi the clear case and belt when Bombay rushed the stage and snatched the mike from Slice's hand.

Screaming that it was a fix and he chose the wrong beats while blaming everyone else for his loss, Bombay then slammed down the microphone and stomped off the stage.

Oh, this is gold, Randall thought. *Photo better get pictures of this.*

When Randall looked around for his photographer, he noticed as Levi was escorted out of the club by the security guards and ushered through a private exit, Bombay was still fuming in the back of the club, gesticulating in a wild manner to no one in particular, and yelling at the top of his lungs at everyone within earshot.

Randall also noticed that Marcus reappeared and was now within range of Bombay's rant.

Marcus had that now-familiar smile glued to his face.

Randall paid little mind to Marcus, however, as he was also busy writing down notes.

While his head was down, Randall hadn't noticed Detective Barron Wilkinson, himself almost cloaked in complete darkness, stealthily snaking his way through the crowd.

Randall, flipping his notebook closed and packing up his small bag and made his way to the restrooms, where he could call Ivey in relative privacy.

Randall took a wide berth around Bombay and his crew, who were still fuming over the loss.

Bombay threw an evil, malicious stare at Randall, who ignored it in step as he made his way to the restroom. *Hey, I wasn't a judge this time,* Randall thought. *Blame your lyricist, bum.*

Seems Bombay had to go too, but noticing Randall, decided against using the bathroom and instead went through the emergency exit and out to the alleyway which ran adjacent to the bathrooms.

Out in the darkened alleyway, Bombay unzipped his jeans, and, still cursing and shaking his head from his loss, began to wet up the alley floor. Just then, a figure approached from the mouth of the alleyway.

"I'm busy here, man," Bombay said. "You can get into this bullshit club from the front door."

"Oh, I'm getting into some bullshit, but not this club," the figure said while adjusting his own pants. "But I peeped the battle. I liked your lines about dishing out head trauma to bitches that betray you. I thought that shit was pretty clever."

Still facing the alley's wall, Bombay face tensed while his stream of urine sputtered.

Before Bombay could process the situation and form any response, his attacker assumed a position directly behind him and grabbed a fistful of the braids which ran down Bombay's neck, before repeatedly rammed Bombay's forehead into the wall.

Each impact echoed with the sound of cracked bone and tearing flesh, muted only somewhat by the smattering of blood.

Over and over again, after each crunching thud, Bombay's attacker mashed and grinded the front of Bombay's head in the wall.

After the fifth and final thrust, Bombay's body slid, mutilated face-first, down the urine-strewn wall, tilting and then falling sideways into a pool of his own piss.

Bombay's body writhed with cadaveric spasms as the last bit of life seeped from his mashed head.

Bombay's killer stepped back to admire his artwork: there was a crimson pulpy lump on the wall, which was the beginning of a gruesome smear of blood and brain matter that formed an unsightly U-Turn that led halfway down to Bombay's mangled and barely recognizable face.

After rifling the dead rapper's pockets, the killer rolled up Bombay's own pocket money and stuffed the billfold deep into Bombay's lifeless mouth.

The sickening thuds startled Randall, who ran from the restrooms and through the exit and out to the alley, only to glimpse Bombay's crumpled body slumped against the wall, as if his corpse was literally tossed there.

The commotion also drew the attention of Splice, a cameraman and two security guards, who were among the first to hit the hallway leading to the back alley. As Randall moved into get a closer look, the swelling crowd behind him pushed Randall face-first into Bombay's bloody and distorted body.

Randall's knees slid through a small puddle of Bombay's blood, urine and bits of skull, hair and brain matter, and he instinctively used his hands to brace his fall. Once on his feet, it was immediately obvious that Randall himself had become a part of the crime scene.

Space and time seemed at once interlocked and frozen.

Randall's eyes went from his hands to his smeared jeans, to his shirt, back to his hands and finally, to the faces of several of the panicked and trauma-stricken people in the crowd.

Randall felt his pulse slowing and his head beginning to swim, and an eerie feeling of weightlessness enveloped his being as his hearing became muffled. Then, blackness.

Randall passed out.

*****

RANDALL must've been out for several minutes, but when he came to, he realized he was laying on one of the couches in the greenroom. Laying down, he moved to sit up and heard the unmistakable sound of friction that ruffled denim makes when caked with dried blood.

Randall's head pounded as he righted himself on the greenroom sofa and slowly began take in his current state and immediate surroundings. He looked at the back of hands, which were still covered with some of Bombay's blood, as were Randall's jacket and sneakers.

Randall reached up and touched his face, which he noticed felt taut, as if some sort of liquid had dried on it and tightened his pores. In a detached way, Randall glanced past the rushing paramedics and crowd of police officers and at his image reflecting back to him from the mirror attached to the restroom's door.

Randall was able to now see his top half in full.

Instead of being shocked at his state, Randall sighed in a way that signified his sense of indifferent acceptance.

Randall stared at his altogether sad and tattered image until he eyeballed an arriving Detective Barron Wilkinson, who was approaching on a very determined and straight path.

Barron looked down at Randall and sighed.

"You want to tell me what happened?" Barron said as he waved over a uniformed officer and a medic. "We know you were among the first on the scene." Randall couldn't tell if the detective was questioning him more out of concern for his case and couldn't care less about Randall's actual mental and physical welfare.

Well, no shit I was one of the first here, Randall sneered to himself. *How do you think I earned all these trophies?*

Randall tried to speak, but had trouble forcing out anything audible. He noticed that his voice became raspy and hoarse, and that his esophagus felt as if it were on fire.

"I was in one of the bathrooms when I heard some very loud like, thuds," Randall finally said while attempting to stand, only for the paramedic and detective to motion for Randall to stay seated. "I just ran towards the sounds, which by the way it sounded, had to be very close. The thuds sounded like…like bones breaking.

"So, I jetted out to the alley and that's when I saw Bombay. I think I must've slipped or something, but the next thing I know, I'm sitting here smelling of shit and piss and I see you coming."

Randall and Barron simultaneously looked at each other with equally conspiratorial stares before the detective filled in some of the blanks, all while Randall's headache thumped on.

"At that point, you apparently passed out and fell right into the murder scene; the deejay and one of the guards carried you the sofa," Barron said. "You took a pretty bad stumble there, Randall; it's a good thing you didn't land directly on your face and head."

Randall again reached up and touched his face, and noticed the right side was slightly swollen. Randall then slowly looked back up at Barron and the medic, who was busy withdrawing a small and shiny tool from his pocket.

The medic kneeled down.

"Sir, look here, please."

With a click, the medic beamed a pole of focused light into each of Randall's eyes, and asked him to follow his finger and if Randall knew who he was, where he was and how he got there.

Randall rolled and blinked his eyes while satisfying the medic that he indeed had all of his wits and faculties about him.

"Of course, doc. I'm fine, I'm fine," Randall said, once again moving to sit up.

"Yeah, he should be good to go," the medic said to the detective before stepping off. "But Mr. Jenkins, be sure to get checked out with your primary; it's important you follow up with your doctor, as you may suffer some pain or other issues later."

Before Randall could rise all the way from the coach, Barron put both hands out, palms down.

"Randall, we are going to need all your clothes from tonight; and we need them right now," Barron said. "You are a very much a literal walking crime scene. That means we need your jacket, shirt, t-shirt, boxers, shoes, socks, hat and any jewelry you have on your person.

"We need everything you have, except your cell phone."

For the first time in a very long time, Randall felt trapped. And strangely, he liked it.

"Crime scene is going to come over and check you out before you strip the dirty clothes," Barron continued, oddly calling the clothes dirty, which was street lingo for the clothes a perpetrator wears when committing a crime. Randall smiled on the inside when he put that 1+1 together. "Is there someone you can call to bring you some fresh clothes and drive you home? If not, one of our units has some general release items that may fit."

Randall sighed. There was only one person he could call.

Chapter Six

RANDALL was unusually calm when, still seated on the sofa and within earshot of Detective Barron Wilkinson, he pulled out his cell phone and touched Ivey's image on the speed dial.

Ivey obviously hadn't heard the news and was in a generally pissed-off mood because Randall was just now calling. Ivey's podcast session had ended some time ago, and she has been at Randall's apartment for three hours before finally hearing from him.

"Damn baby, I was beginning to worry about you. Fuck you at?"

"I am sitting in the greenroom at Soco's, covered in Bombay's blood and talking to Detective Wilkinson," Randall said in deadpan manner. "Bombay was killed tonight, and I sort of fell into it. Anyway, I need you to bring me a clean layup, because I was asked to surrender my clothes."

As his statement was met with a loud silence, Randall realized he may have left out a crucial detail.

"I didn't kill him, Ivey," Randall said, letting out a little chuckle at hearing the absurdity that came out of his own mouth. "But it is a messy, fucked up situation."

Ivey had long ago and much earlier in the conversation dropped the spliff she was smoking, which was now smoldering on the floor. Her eyes bulged and grew glossy before a burst of tears drained down her face.

"Oh my god…oh my god," Ivey stammered and repeated. "How and…what? What? Bombay is what and what? Oh my god, I'm on my way."

The shakes ravaged Ivey's body as a frosty bolt shot down her spine, momentarily freezing her tailbone to the edge of the bed. Ivey blinked several times and wiped her face before springing to action.

Ivey darted through Randall's dresser and grabbed a pair of sweatpants and a matching pullover hoodie, some socks and a pair of Nike slides. She knew that Randall would only need enough clothes to walk from Soco's to her forest-green RAV-4, and from her car to his apartment.

Knowing Randall, he'll probably take four showers, all at once, Ivey thought, which brought a faint smile to her face.

Swiping there still burning spliff from the floor, Ivey grabbed her ever-present go bag and car keys and was on her way to Soco's.

After hanging up with Ivey, Randall looked at up at the detective, who acted as if he weren't eavesdropping on Randall's conversation, although both he and the detective knew that he was.

"Okay, I called, and my people are bringing me some clothes and are going to take me back to my spot," Randall said, this time not trying to get up. Instead, Randall settled back into the couch. "No what, detective?"

Mentioning the word call, Randall noticed he hasn't yet heard from anyone at the paper, including the photographer.

Barron directed a nearby officer to post up by the restrooms and motioned for Randall to stand.

"Use that restroom to take off your clothes. We ask that you take your time and use extreme care when you strip down," Barron said. "You can undo as many buttons as you need to comfortably get out of the clothes, but once you do, do not fold them nor arrange them in any way. We want to preserve as much evidence as possible, so the less you disturb your clothing from this point on, the better. I'll let you know when your folks arrive."

So, this is what this feels like when this happens, Randall thought as he slowly rose and took what felt like wide-legged baby steps toward the restroom, his headache booming with each stride.

Once in the restroom, which doubled as a smaller dressing room for when the main changing rooms were occupied, Randall flipped on both light switches and for the first time was able to get a full body look at himself in restroom's inner full-length mirror.

Randall slowly looked down at his hands before raising his palms. While Randall was unconscious, the medic had apparently taken antiseptic wipes to Randall's face, forehead and hands, because his palms were extraordinarily clean and dry, even by Randall's standards.

Randall continued staring at his likeness as it also raised its hand to its scalp, mimicking Randall's movements. Randall's fingers stopped at his hairline when he felt his hair which grew stiff from absorbing some of Bombay's leaked body fluids.

Randall suddenly felt heavy, like he was saddled with lightweight workout straps.

Taking another step back to get more of his whole body in the mirror, Randall had a macabre revelation: he felt heavier because his clothes soaked up that much of Bombay.

Randall almost dry-heaved as he gingerly stripped down and felt relieved to remove the soiled clothes that he hoped to never see them again.

Somehow, even Randall's boxers were damp.

Now naked, Randall slowly made his way forward to the sink and ran hot water over his hands.

Taking the bar of Ivory from its dish, Randall scrubbed his hands together until they grew raw, and did the same with his face, careful not to aggravate the swollen right side.

It took some doing for the Randall to finally rinse the antiseptic from his face and to clear his nose, but when he was finished, Randall regretted it, as a wave of nausea churned through his gut.

Randall noticed it was the smell. Not only the smell of death. No, Randall was used to the smell of death, but after the fact, like the smell when a funeral home is dressing the body of the deceased. This was a smell of *fresh* death, of new blood.

Randall reached for the sink to steady and brace himself in case he lost the fight with this new and revolting fetor emanating from the pile of bloodied clothes.

Just outside, Ivey barely had time to park before she bounded through Soco's entrance.

Ivey was moving fast enough to elude the grip of the two officers at the door.

"Where is Randall?" Ivey yelled. "My name is Ivey Stewart, and I have his clothes and I'm taking him home."

As the two officers grabbed Ivey, she instinctively snatched her arm away and again demanded to see Randall. By that time, most of the attention turned to the screaming young lady holding some clothes.

That's my angel, Randall thought to himself, as he, too, could hear Ivey's loud demand.

Barron reached Ivey and the officers before the situation could escalate.

"My name is Detective Barron Wilkinson, and I am the lead on this case," Barron said to a still-simmering Ivey. "I understand you are here for Mr. Jenkins. I will take these items to him, and we should be done with him in just a short while."

Frustrated but not wanting to agitate matters, Ivey reluctantly followed Barron's outstretched hand to the couch that Randall occupied no more than 45 minutes ago. Ivey's body language radiated dissatisfaction as she sat on the couch and crossed her legs. She then pulled out her cell phone and typed out several messages.

Randall, relieved to hear Ivey's voice, turned his head away from the clothes and inhaled in two short sniffs as he made his way to the door to alert the guard that he did as instructed and now needed his fresh clothes. The officer silently obliged by handing Randall his clothes through the short clearance above the restroom's door.

Now dressed well enough for public consumption, Randall again knocked on the door to let the officer know he was coming out. Ivey sprung to her feet when she saw Randall and rushed by Barron and the officer and gave Randall a hug so tight, he had to gasp.

Randall felt his body go limp just bit in Ivey's clutches.

Still holding him by the waist, Ivey leaned back to take a look at Randall's face. She then kissed Randall before laying her head on his left shoulder.

"Don't tell this detective a fucking thing," Ivey sweetly whispered into Randall's ear, before gently kissing his earlobe and breaking their embrace.

Randall instantly concluded that to be sage advice.

Ivey was now standing by Randall's side when Detective Barron Wilkinson approached.

Ivey jumped in and commandeered the next move before the detective had a chance to say anything.

"I am taking Randall home," Ivey said in a way that was more of a statement of fact than a request for permission. "You know where he will be if you need to reach him."

Barron was unmoved by Ivey's stance, but relented and decided to play the long game.

"Okay Ms. Stewart, Randall is free to go. But as an eyewitness Randall, know that we will be stopping by soon to ask further questions," Barron said, trying to take the edge out of his voice. "Thank you for all of your help tonight, Randall; and remember to get that lump looked at."

Barron then stepped aside, and the couple weaved their way through the crowd and out to Ivey's SUV.

Randall was glad to be outside and to fill his nostrils with the nighttime Philly air.

Randall's olfactory freedom was short-lived, because Ivey was pulling Randall by the arm to her curbed Toyota. Ivey had to strong-arm her way through a small group of gawkers who assembled on the sidewalk who also knew Randall.

The pair rode in silence as Ivey expedited their trip from the club back to Randall's apartment. Now knowing that Randall was safe, she left Randall in the bathroom, where he stayed for more than 90 minutes. Ivey heard the shower start and stop three times.

Inside the bathroom Randall took turns repeatedly washing his hair, fingernails and body until his skin squeaked.

Randall even took the time to scrub his toenails, as he wanted to make sure he cleansed himself of whatever remained of Bombay. It took longer than what Randall imagined it would to wash Bombay's blood from his hair and the stink of the entire evening from his person.

When finished, Randall left the bathroom and found Ivey sitting on the bed, waiting for him with a look of bottled anticipation. As if on cue, Ivey lit a just-rolled Entourage and passed it to Randall.

"Baby, what the fuck happened?" Ivey inquired as Randall dried off from the shower. The lingering smell of dried blood mixed with body wash and the humidity of a hot shower was new for Randall, but he didn't mind the sweet, pungent odor all that much, all things considering.

"I don't know, baby. The show was over, and it was decisive; Levi really handed Bombay his own ass," Randall said, his hands trembled as he passed that leafy blunt back to Ivey. "Bombay was mad as shit; I side-stepped him while I ran to the bathroom. I was about to call you when I heard these sounds, like a bag of bones being thrown against the wall. I ran out to the back, only to see son bleeding from his head, real fuckin' bad, too.

"I tried to get a closer look, but those fuckin' clowns out there bumped me right into Bombay's body, and that's how I ended up with his shit all over me. Barron told me I passed out."

Randall's voice tailed off during the retelling, and Ivey got up and rubbed his back. "It was real, real nasty."

"This is a fucked-up situation, baby," Ivey said as she relit the Entourage. "Do you need call your editor?"

Randall didn't have a chance to think of what this would mean for him and the paper, but knowing his editors, the paper would probably want to play up the first-hand account of the latest hip-hop murder in the 'hood.

Randall groaned at the thought. *Great.*

Just then his cell phone buzzed, and Randall nodded for Ivey to answer it.

"That was Detective Wilkinson. The cops are on their way to pick you up," Ivey said. "I'm going with you, but just remember to give him your statement and nothing else."

Thoughts of blood and images of Bombay's lifeless eyes blankly staring out from a face that had been contorted and mutilated made Randall ill, and before he could move or summon Ivey for help, he felt an unstoppable, caustic and bitter surge rising in his chest, and his throat began to burn from the oncoming and unmistakable regurgitation of stomach acid that was now shooting up his thorax.

Sensing the explosion, Ivey retrieved the kitchen trashcan and put it under Randall with precious microseconds to spare.

The pain worsened with each heave, until it finally made Randall double over, his face nearly touching his own growing pool of vomit in the pail, which was now streaked with blood from burst capillaries in Randall's throat.

Ivey quickly moved him to the bed and put a cool, damp rag on his forehead, and placed a pillow under his feet.

Randall's head was still swimming when the phone in Randall's apartment rang. Ivey answered the phone on the third ring.

"That was Gretchen on the phone, wanting to know if you were there," Ivey said, her eyes bulging from the weight of the situation and from serving as impromptu point-man for Randall. "I didn't know what to say, baby. I told her you were there, but you are composing yourself and would call her later. She said homicide detectives already called the paper looking for you. I told her we were waiting for a squad car to pick us up."

Seemingly as soon as Ivey informed Randall of Gretchen's phone call, there was an urgent knock at the door, the type of three-rap cadence that could only come from the worn and hardened knuckles of a detective, who was probably with a crew of other detectives.

Ivey answered the door as Randall quickly dressed.

Two very serious looking detectives greeted Randall as he made his way into his living room. Both wore dark-hued suits and looked every bit the part of homicide detectives that knew their way around a killing.

"Thank you for your cooperation," the older detective said while staring straight through Randall. "We only want to go over your statement; it shouldn't take long. We also need any washcloths you may have used, along with the soap and towel."

Randall felt the sudden need for immediate and effective legal representation.

"Should I call my lawyer?" Randall asked, becoming leery about the requests and the mere presence of the detectives, neither of whom Randall has ever seen before during his years of covering crime.

"No, that won't be necessary at all, Mr. Jenkins, but you are free to, of course," the older detective said, now surveying Randall's apartment. "We just have specific questions for you in particular, because we confirmed with your editor that you cover the rap scene in the city and were, in fact, scheduled to cover this particular show."

Randall gnashed his teeth at being sold out by Gretchen.

She can fucking forget about me ever doing a favor for her again, Randall almost muttered aloud.

Out of the corner of his eye, Randall spotted Ivey in the kitchen doorway, eyes wide and mouth agape, slowly shaking her head "no" back and forth.

"You might also want to bring a sweater, as it gets chilly down at the Roundhouse for visitors," the shorter, younger detective said, also peering around the apartment but apparently paying little regard to the tray holding a pack of Backwoods and a half ounce of marijuana.

The mere mention of the notorious street name for police headquarters shot yet another chill up Randall's spine. Even as a reporter, Randall hated stepping foot in that place; it just gave him bad vibes. "Don't worry, Mr. Jenkins. You will be fine."

The older detective opened the front door in a manner that beckoned Randall and Ivey to gather their things and leave. Locking the door, Randall and Ivey now found themselves sandwiched between the two detectives as they headed down the steps and out to the awaiting black Crown Victoria.

Driving that Crown Victoria was Detective Barron Wilkinson.

"Mr. Jenkins, I wish we could have continued our conversation under better circumstances," Barron said. "You and I have a lot to discuss."

*****

THE Roundhouse, a building shaped in the form of a pair of handcuffs, was deemed outmoded the moment it was built by architect Robert Louis Geddes and his firm way back in 1962. From then until recently, it stood, along with the infamous maximum-security Graterford Prison, as the bookends to Philadelphia's judicial system. It was long held that if you entered the Roundhouse, your only exit was through Graterford.

Now Randall and Ivey were in the back seat of the black Crown Victoria, as all five occupants - Barron, Randall, Ivey and the other two detectives - sat in deafening silence as Barron maneuvered the squad car down Arch Street.

The Roundhouse seemed to rise from the depths of the horizon, and Randall wondered if this was the view and feeling experienced by soon-to-be convicts.

Randall instinctively squeezed Ivey's hand as Barron whipped the car into a spot marked "Reserved - Detectives" in the Roundhouse's open-air parking lot and turned off the car.

As the other detectives exited but before Randall and Ivey could get out, Barron turned to them. Staring.

"Ms. Stewart, you can leave. As we said, we really just need to talk to Randall," Barron said in an unbelievably considerate tone. "We already know you weren't there, and that you can provide little material value as it relates to our investigation. My team of detectives were a bit…aggressive in the pick-up, and that is because they know I like to be very, very thorough. Of course, you can stay with Randall, but this may take several hours."

Randall vised Ivey's palm hard enough to crush all five metacarpal bones in her right hand. Ivey got the point of that silent missive.

"A few hours? Thank you, Detective Wilkinson, but if you need Randall, then I need to be with him. But you only need this statement and for him to answer a few questions, right? In that case, he should be able to leave whenever he wants."

The smile that crept on Barron's face struck Randall as being familiar.

Randall respected the undeniable sensation of his blood pouring to his feet, leaving him briefly lightheaded. "Of course, Randall can leave whenever he wants," Barron lied. "Again, we only want his statement, personal physical effects, which we already have, and to just ask him a few more questions. Trust me."

Randall was all too familiar with the Roundhouse and it's too-small parking lot and antiquated amenities.

Wilkinson waved his party through the twin sets of metal detectors and toward the far right elevator, marked and reserved for police department personnel. Swiping his ID card, Barron called for the elevator and stood silently, peering over to Randall and then Ivey. Ivey picked up on it, and then decided to question *him.*

Ivey pinched her eyes as she looked at Barron's blurred reflection in the brushed aluminum exterior paneling of the closed elevator door.

"So, why did you really leave New York? Too much curry for you?" Ivey said. "You were pretty popular up there."

Randall couldn't believe the balls on Ivey. And apparently, neither could Barron, although he remained stoic.

"New York. That was a good time; they just weren't ready for my methods. But there is no better feeling than getting killers and drug dealers off the street. Wouldn't you agree, Randall?" Barron said as the arriving elevator pinged, ending its descent from the third floor. "See, that is my thing; I don't care whose feelings get hurt, as long as the case gets closed."

"By any means necessary, apparently," Ivey mumbled, but in a way that everyone could hear it. As the elevator door opened, Barron turned to face Ivey, full-body style. "I do what needs to be done, Ms. Stewart. It is what I do, and rest assured, I don't lose any sleep over it."

With that, Barron stepped into the open yet exceedingly cramped elevator, swiped his card against a digital security scanner and stood inside expectantly, waiting for Ivey and Randall to join him.

"Let's go," Barron said, in a tone that left little room for debate. Ivey and Randall looked at one another, and with a deep breath, they both got in to take the trip upstairs with Barron.

The seven-second ride up seemed an eternity for the claustrophobic Randall.

The trio exited on the third floor and into a section of the Roundhouse that Randall has never seen. The old-school wood-paneled hallways branched off and gave way to state-of-the-art suites and detective offices.

Barron led Randall and Ivey at a brisk pace, as many detectives looked up and stared at the trio. Randall sensed that he might not be able to leave when he wanted to, after all.

Just as Randall was about to question Barron on that issue, the detective made a sharp left turn toward a frosted glass door marking the office as belonging to one Detective Barron Wilkinson.

With yet another swipe of his ID card, the door unlocked, and Barron went in first. No formalities or niceties this time, as Barron didn't bother holding the door nor inviting the pair in.

Ivey entered first. Randall took his time before entering the detective's office, instead absorbing the surroundings and formidable environment.

Randall entered and eased his way into one of two rickety Lorne chairs that stood in stark contrast to the buttery-soft leather of the Issey-designed chair that reigned behind Barron's desk.

Randall took in the various awards hanging on the walls, and for a second, had the thought that a detective with Barron's pedigree should have at least triple the amount of awards. Randall took particular note of the absence of a desk phone.

Tellingly, Randall spotted the rather prestigious "Officer of the Year Award," which Barron received from the National Rifle Association for his work in New York with the anti-organized crime unit.

Guess that 'hip-hop cop' shit paid off, Randall thought, as a sneer crept across his face.

Ivey was sneering too, but directly at Barron, who casually threw himself into the off-white leather chair, which clashed with the rest of his office.

"Well, here we are," Ivey said, without breaking eye contact with Barron. "What can Randall do for you to make it easier for you to do your job, detective?"

Randall bristled internally at Ivey's consistent pricking of Barron; the detective, in an obvious affront to hierarchy, protocol and the numerous hazards and laws involved - leaned back, opened the top left drawer of his desk, and extracted a pack of Camel Turkish Royals cigarettes.

Randall and Ivey sat in muted awe and disbelief as Wilkinson opened the pack, took one out, reached into his suit jacket and pulled out a solid gold lighter and lit the unique blend. Just then, Randall recalled that Barron also smoked Newports.

The pair looked at each other and then back at Barron just in time to observe the detective taking a full drag.

Barron's exhaust and how natural the movement seemed was not lost on Ivey.

That's the pull of a longtime weed smoker, Ivey thought. *I wonder who he gets his weed from.*

After a second long and elaborate pull on his cigarette, Barron reached in the same drawer and retrieved a fancy ashcup, and gently tapped his cigarette in it. Barron's whole behavior was slow and deliberate, as if he was purposefully trying to unnerve his guests.

Although the sweet-smelling tobacco blend was strong and immediately filled his office, the detective remained unbothered about what his peers and higher-ups might say.

No officer batted an eye at Barron's apparent mockery of established non-smoking ordinances.

Apparently, *these* investigators on *this* floor of the Roundhouse were free to smoke as they wish.

Randall wondered what else they were free to do - or get away with. *Probably lots of really grimy, scary shit,* Randall concluded.

The detective took two more puffs from his cigarette before once again tapping the embers inside the cup.

After what seemed an eternity, Barron tossed peering looks at Randall and then Ivey.

"Okay, I'll put it straight out to the both of you: we believe, and I should say I know, that Randall knows more about these two murders than he is letting on. We find that Randall has an incredible knack for being in the wrong place at the right time, or Temple's journalism school should make him professor emeritus," Barron said, his words dripping with condescension. "How do you explain your knack for being on scene at two straight murders at these clubs? In addition, you also knew both of the slain rappers."

Randall felt a pang of something not quite foreign but rare in his adult life: fear. But unlike in previous encounters with this sensation, Randall found himself aroused by this confrontation; not with the detective, but with the fear, which is what Barron provided at that very moment.

"Simple. Because we in the newsroom have these things called 'scanners,' which allows us to eavesdrop on real-time police calls and get there long before you guys show up; and believe it or not, we all have sources in, what do you call it, the ''hood'? yeah, we have sources there, who are often more reliable than your jailhouse snitches," Randall shot back in a tone sharp enough to startle Ivey and cause Barron to withdraw back in his seat. "See, I guess Temple's journalism program taught me something after all. Now c'mon with all this bullshit, detective."

Now it was Ivey's turn to wrench Randall's hand to try to get him to calm down and realize the gravity of the situation. But for Randall, when angry, the wrong thing to do was to try to calm him down. Doing so only fueled Randall's hostility and put him even more on the offensive.

"Nah, what is it, rap cop; what is your real beef?" Randall continued, digging his heels into Barron.

"What, you think one of these rappers out here are now killing other rappers? Don't you have footage, eyewitnesses and all that shit?"

Ivey was caught somewhere between rigor mortis and awe: deathly afraid of what the police were capable of in these offices which seemed cut off from the rest of the crime-fighting world, and also astonished at Randall's fully erect backbone.

Barron, however, was unmoved; the detective has seen and heard this act before.

Instead of meeting Randall's fire with fire of his own, Barron met it with the cool haze of his still-burning Turkish cigarette.

"Relax. Of course, we have eyewitnesses, surveillance, and cell phone footage; we even have a statement from Ben fucking Franklin, but that still doesn't answer my question now, does it?" Barron countered. "The last two murders, you were either present or were the first reporter there. Please, explain."

Fuck that. The last time I tried to explain some shit, I ended up on the wrong end of a lawsuit in my rookie year at the paper, Randall thought, as his mind simultaneously plotted his next move in this chess game. *So, this is for damn sure; I don't know anything, and even if I did, I'm not telling this lame-ass detective a thing.*

"No, I don't think it needs to be explained any further than I already explained it. The events I cover are part of my gig; of course I'm going to get there early and have some sort of access," Randall said. "If a crime happens and I'm there, then of course my editors are going to want the story. What about all the other assaults and shootings in clubs that I never attended or wrote about? Are you going to ask me about them or are you, you know, going to get around to doing your job?"

Barron titled his head in that way one does when contemplating what to say, while trying to also talk himself out of saying what he really wanted to say. What the detective really wanted to say is that Randall is now officially a person of interest, or at the least, an important material witness. But Randall was neither. Not officially. Not yet.

"Glad you've gotten all that out of your system. What else did Temple teach you?" Barron stated more than he asked.

"It also taught me to cherish and exercise my rights, which I will do right now by informing you that if you have any more questions, you can ask them to my lawyer," Randall said while rising from his chair. "Pretty good, that Temple."

Ivey, battling with a temporary case of advanced chronic laryngitis, mutely followed suit and rose from her chair.

Barron knew he couldn't keep Randall, and he didn't want to goose Randall into tumbling on to the fact that he on Barron's short list of prime suspects. The detective needed to keep Randall just close enough, but at arm's distance.

"As I said earlier, we don't need to get any lawyers involved," the detective said through a forced, yet practiced easy face while dabbing out the cigarette and rising from his chair as well.

"Don't mind my questioning; innocent people usually react the way you have thus far. But listen, the department and I, just like the two of you, want this killer caught. I mean, it is only going to be a matter of time before these sorts of high-profile murders lead to a near-complete shutdown of lucrative underground hip-hop as you know it; believe me on this."

Barron's words came across to Randall as a warning from a formidable adversary.

"And I don't want to see any more of these rappers killed, and I certainly don't want someone innocent taking the rap.

"So, let's work together," Barron added while opening the door to his office to lead Randall and Ivey back to the elevator. "If you hear anything, please let me know. And who knows? Maybe I can throw a tip or two your way."

Ivey produced an audible smirk at Barron's parting remark; Randall, however, was happy to be out of the detective's office. Just as when the pair arrived, Randall and Ivey again trailed Barron by several footsteps as he led them back to the bank of elevators. Only this time, they were going to take "public" elevator down.

Ivey and Randall remained silent as they reached the Roundhouse lobby, and speed-walked past the outsized security desk and through the double-door exit.

It was only at that moment when Randall felt he could truly exhale. Doing so, he glanced at Ivey, who was staring at Randall with a look that contained some mixture of bewilderment, reverence and anger.

Anger, though, would win out and emerge first.

Randall sensed the outburst coming as they strode through the parking lot and toward the El stop at 8th and Market St.

Ivey didn't erupt often, but when she did, Randall could sense the oncoming explosion better than a veteran volcanologist surveying Kilauea.

"Randall, what the fuck was THAT? Why would you try to antagonize him like that? I understand that you were tired of his shit, but you probably made things worse," Ivey said with a tone that was quite heavy on bass and high on treble. "He's going to go out of his way to make trouble for you and the paper now."

Inside that very moment, Randall had the damnedest of thoughts: *fuck Barron. And fuck his investigation and fuck the paper for bending over for him. But right now, fuck you, Ivey.*

Randall tried and often failed at his attempts a being a calm person who lived by the principle that one person has to think with a clear head when two people are arguing. But he was not going to take being undressed like this in public. Not by Barron. Not by anyone, not even Ivey.

"First, never fucking scream on me like that again. Second, you think I give two shits about Barron now? He'll come up with some suspect and the department will either solve it, or not," Randall said with a particular edge in his voice that captured every bit of Ivey's attention. "Everybody wants to fade on me. I have no doubt that my job sold me out to Barron, and now here you go, telling me I need to just kiss his ass and play nice. You, of all people, telling me to do that."

That was another of Randall's issues. While he exhibited resolute loyalty, there was a reason why Randall was more of a loner; he expected the same sort of blood in, blood out loyalty from the people he did let into his inner circle, and would react harshly - sometimes, most times, overreacting - to what he felt was a breach of that loyalty.

And right then, Randall believed that Ivey was coming irrevocably close to breaking that principle.

Ivey, however, took a moment to breathe before returning fire. And it was then that she decided to reset her clapper to safety, and to instead offer a dove of sorts.

"Baby, you know better than to ever question my loyalty, and that I would never turn on you. But this all just…so overwhelming for me right now; I mean, that's two people we both knew, killed in less than three days. I hate to see you like this; to see you act like this," Ivey said, while gripping Randall's arm, forcing him to stop walking and turn to face her.

Randall saw legit fear and concern on her face, and also that she was hurt by his words. "I feel like this detective is going to try to jam you somehow with these killings, and you're going to lose everything because of this cop, who obviously has his dick upright, just for you."

The realist inside of Randall knew that Ivey was right. Sighing, he gave her a strong hug and felt like shit for blasting his one true partner.

"I know baby, and I'm sorry. I should have never came at you like that," Randall gently whispered into Ivey's ear. "I'm scared, too. But there are several things that I do know. One, Barron can look at me all he wants; the simple fact is, he will be wasting his time, as the only thing I have in common with these events is that I attended one event and was assigned to cover the other. Two, I'm done cooperating with Barron. Next time he questions me, he had better be in the company of a warrant of some sort. And third? Well baby, you're on my side; I can't lose, right?"

Randall then gently pecked Ivey's left cheek, which made her blush, just a bit.

"You think you can smooth-talk your way into and out of anything, don't you?" Ivey said as she playfully pulled away from Randall's embrace. "That's how you got into these panties to begin with."

That remark made Randall truly laugh out loud, and when he caught up with Ivey, she produced a nicely rolled entourage, specially packed for transportation. Randall was flabbergasted - and impressed.

"No shit; when did you have a chance to put that together, and did you have that with you through the whole time?" Randall asked incredulously, although he knew the answer to both questions. As a rule, Ivey always carried an "emergency" go bag - which included a rolled pink Entourage, matches, a pack of gum and two Septa tokens. "See, that's why I'm with you, you always think ahead."

Ivey smiled and winked, her eyes glistening in the evening light. "Hey, I've been taught by the best," Ivey said, after lighting the flared end of the entourage and deeply inhaling, and then exhaling, the aromatic vapor. "And besides, I knew you would need to burn a tree to melt off that bullshit with Barron. And I also knew that they wouldn't do a serious pat-down at the station, since we were being escorted in by Barron and two plainclothes.

"Yeah, I took a chance that we'd have the dumb luck of bumping into a K-9 unit, but even if they sniffed us out?" Ivey said, before bowing her head in an elaborate manner while placing her hand over her heart. "'Mea Culpa; the detectives startled and rushed us, and in the confusion, I picked up the wrong bag. You can give me a summons for this little bit of weed, though.'"

Ivey then flashed a hilarious full-mouth grin at Randall before passing him the entourage. It was like her face turned into a deep chocolate version of that wide-smile emoji. Randall loved it.

Taking the blunt and also inhaling deeply, holding and then exhaling, Randall's mind was allowed a brief moment of escapism, away from the bullshit that was these killings, Barron's investigation, the job; everything.

Randall and Ivey walked in a happy near-silence as they zig-zagged through tiny Old City blocks on their way to 5th and Market, deciding since they were indeed smoking, that it would be best if they head toward the El stop that had less foot traffic for their recreational purposes.

Approaching the stop at 8th and Market, they believed, would be far too busy for them to properly enjoy their traveling herbs.

Like a well-rehearsed script barreling towards its predictable finish, the pink entourage had just been singed into a no longer useful burnt end, which Ivey casually flicked to the curb.

"On point, right?" Ivey said, again flashing that mischievous smile while digging out a pack of gum. "Hopefully, it helped you forget about that fucking cop, if but for a moment."

"Did it ever, baby; you know I needed that. I need something else, too, though," Randall replied, tugging at Ivey's waist. The coupled laughed it up as they approached the stairwell to the El at 5th Street, but Randall's laugh was caught mid-throat, as he glanced across the street and swore he saw a recognizable silhouette limp down the steps of the opposite subway portal.

After pausing a moment to watch the figure disappear into the entrance, Randall shrugged it off and rejoined Ivey and together, they descended the bi-level stairwell which was adorned with historical paintings, reflective of the historic district served by the stop at 5th and Market.

Using the last of the no-longer circulated tokens, Ivey paid the fare for both herself and Randall, and they waited for the oncoming train. It looked like Ivey had no plans on going to her apartment and had every intention of going back and staying the night at Randall's place, which was fine enough with Randall, as he damn sure could use the company. From where they were, it was probably easier to just go back to Randall's place anyway.

"So, what do you think happen now?" Ivey asked as they found a pair of open seats in the third car of the train, which was unusually packed for such a late hour. "You have a plan?"

"I didn't think I needed a plan, baby; I didn't do anything wrong, the cops have what they need from me, and I'm sure the paper would love to hear my account of what just went down," Randall said, while concurrently thinking *oh yeah, and fuck them again for diming me out to Barron.* "But my immediate plan is to get back to my apartment with you, shower, chill and call my editor. They will just have to wait for this to run in Wednesday's edition or on the web; after that, I just want to put this bullshit behind us, at least for tonight."

Back at the Roundhouse and long after Randall and Ivey departed, Detective Barron Wilkinson stood at the elevator, staring at the matte silver elevator door. Beyond being stupefied by Randall's sassier audacity, Barron also found himself concerned about Ivey's well-being and couldn't shake the feeling that she may be in danger.

But that sentiment would have to wait, because Barron's first priority was finding out more about his own prime suspect and coping with the realization that he was running out of time.

Chapter Seven

AFTER Randall and Ivey's meeting with Detective Barron Wilkinson ended just after midnight Tuesday, Marcus watched as the couple teeter-tottered down 6th Street in a giggle-inducing post-smoke haze.

Marcus didn't want to waste any time. After all, it's been a minute since he caught up to his friend.

Unnoticed by Randall, Marcus seamlessly made his way across the free interchange crosswalk connecting the trains traveling in opposite directions; Marcus then slid through the crowd and stood just a few feet away from the pair as they joined a throng of people waiting to board the oncoming West Philly-bound El.

Marcus decided to wait before surprising Randall, and instead sat in an empty seat a row behind the couple.

Marcus was far enough away that Randall would never see him. Besides, Marcus knew that he and Randall would link up soon, so he decided to let his man chill with his lady on the ride home.

Still, Marcus had to chuckle when he eavesdropped on their conversation; he was fascinated that Randall was stumped by the whodunit.

Stifling himself, Marcus nearly doubled over in laughter while listening as Randall surmised the person who knocked off Streaks and then Bombay had to either be working with someone or was a certified solo lunatic badass - or both.

Marcus sat in bemused silence for the duration of the lovebirds' trip on the El, and when they got off at 34th Street, Marcus made sure to exit from the middle doors and slid through the exit turnstile before

Randall and Ivey had the chance to do the same.

Marcus walked along the sidewalk on the opposite side of the street and followed the unaware couple as they made their way to Randall's apartment.

*****

IVEY slowly stroked Randall's brow as he slept in her arms, a sense of worry sweeping over her. Even before this recent string of murders, Ivey was always worried about his well-being and emotional state. It was now Wednesday morning; four days after Streaks' murder, three days after Bombay's killing and two days since Detective Barron Wilkinson questioned Randall.

Was it the nature of his job? Was it the stress of covering both crimes and music? Was it all starting to get to him? Ivey mulled silently. Something has definitely changed in Randall, and Ivey fretted over her lover.

At Ivey's urging, Randall decided to take Tuesday off and spend some time at Ivey's place, which would give him a chance to get himself together for Wednesday's assignment.

Gretchen, however, told Randall that she wanted to meet with him as soon as he reached the newsroom.

Reaching over to grab the leftover blunt in the crystal ashtray (a tongue-in-cheek gift that Randall had purchased as a gift on the first anniversary of them being a couple), Ivy, doing her best to not disturb Randall, lit it and took a long, quiet pull.

Like a resting shark that can still smell a drop of blood in the waters dozens of miles away, Randall woke up and caught Ivey in mid-exhale.

"Good morning baby; sleep well?" inquired Ivey, passing Randall the blunt.

"Of course, baby, and what better way to wake up?" Randall said.

Randall took the lit Entourage from Ivey and took two quick pulls before handing it back. He felt Ivey's trepidation, and worked to ease her thoughts. With everything going on, the couple barely had any time at all to discuss Wednesday's hip-hop showcase at the Liacouras Center on Temple's main campus. The event would also serve as an official album release party for Frostman, a rapper from Germantown.

"Baby, I know and can see how you feel. Don't worry about any bullshit popping off tonight; it's at the Liacouras Center, and you know that thing is going to be outfitted with every Temple cop and cops from the district," Randall said while standing up to stretch. "Shit, I'm more concerned about my check-in with Gretchen."

The sheer mention of Gretchen's name instantly brought to mind the conversation he was to have with his editor later. Gretchen seemed cool with everything going on, and gave the impression she was more than satisfied with Randall's spot coverage of these murders on the circuit. But the more Randall thought about it, the more concerned he became.

Gretchen, for all her qualities, was a stickler for adhering to deadlines, and once she has her eyes set on a story, reporters should be prepared to go through certain extremes to produce.

So even though Randall's past few days were totally fucked up and he was incredibly exhausted from the meeting with Barron, Gretchen still expected him to file that story remotely.

"Just throw something together," Gretchen said then. "And if anything breaks, you can file a follow-up when you get in on Wednesday."

Randall's thoughts continued as he showered in Ivey's decidedly cultural and feminist bathroom.

Outfitted with OPP shower curtains emblazoned with the catchphrase from Naughty By Nature's timeless hip-hop anthem, and bathroom mats adorned with a repeating yellow-lettered "W," an homage to her favorite group the Wu-Tang Clan, Ivey's bathroom was sort of mini hip-hop museum.

Painted in a pale lilac color, it also had a toilet seat cover with the picture of a Technic 1200 turntable; the tissue dispenser was and old-school hand carved piece of a naked soul sister with a giant afro which dispensed paper through her open hands; Ivey's mirror featured ivy vines climbing up from the base of the mirror and meeting again at the top of it.

Randall was always amazed at Ivey's touch for decorating.

As the steam enveloped and then totally fogged the mirror, Randall thought more of tonight's show and his meeting with Gretchen.

Gretchen always had the knack of a requiring a by-the-minute rundown of the events Randall covered, and lately, she has become even more hands-on, given the rising violence on the scene. In some ways, Randall was surprised that Gretchen was not only fine with him attending these events, but enjoyed the small uptick in readership, due in no small part to Randall's coverage.

All Randall had to do was show up, grab a seat, take some notes and be out. *In and out,* Randall muttered to himself, laughing at the obvious lie. Because it has never been in and out at any of these shows, and Randall seemed to be hanging out around these venues more than before.

The Liacouras Center hosted its fair share of concerts, and usually, there's no drama whatsoever. It also mattered that the police have begun to ramp up their patrols of Temple's campus to the point where now, you couldn't flick a burnt end without hitting a Temple University Public Safety Officer.

Randall searched his mind for the last time there were a shooting or other such violence following an event at the center and could only come up with a brawl that happened after a boxing match. Aside from that, Randall couldn't think of any other incidences.

Drying off and wrapping himself in one of Ivey's Rita Marley towels, Randall cracked the bathroom door to allow some of the steam to escape.

Randall took a hard look at himself in the mirror. Randall noticed little wrinkles beginning to form around his eyes, and that his beard was coming in a touch raggedy.

Out of habit, Randall inched closer and closer to the mirror, again bringing his nose within a hair of the image staring back at him. Through some inner compulsion, Randall titled his head to the left, and watched as the image also tilted its head.

Randall then quickly titled his head to the right, and for a split-second, Randall thought the image was a moment or two too slow in mimicking his moves.

"Gotcha," Randall whispered, chuckling at the image, which chuckled back.

Ivey, well out of earshot, watched as Randall analyzed himself in the mirror.

This isn't the first time Ivey spied Randall talking to himself in the mirror. At first, Ivey wasn't worried, and chalked it up to one of Randall's quirks. But lately, Randall seemed to be doing it more often - and talking to himself for longer spots of time.

Ivey filed that in her mind and gently smiled at Randall, who met her eyes after concluding his mirror chat.

"You have the softest eyes," Randall said. "But they always tell on you."

Ivey had to laugh. "Oh yeah, Sherlock? What am I thinking right now?"

"That you must've hooked up with one crazy dude who likes to talk to himself in the mirror." Randall smiled at Ivey as her eyes indeed betrayed her. "Don't worry baby; I'm just giving myself the once over and making sure I'm still sane."

With that, Randall exited the bathroom, kissed Ivey on the forehead and retrieved his clothes from her closet.

Randall always kissed Ivey on the forehead after showering, which was Ivey's cue to roll a fresh Entourage while she watched him get dressed. She always took this moment to enjoy the reverse strip show.

Since Ivey didn't spin on Wednesdays, she had no reason to get up and get dressed, and instead continued lounging in panties and snug t-shirt. As Randall finished dressing, Ivey lit the blunt and passed it to Randall.

"So, what do you think of this meeting with Gretchen? I think she has a thing for you," Ivey said, gently elbowing Randall in the ribs. "Am I going to lose you to your editor? You know I'll beat a bitch up for you, right?" Ivey then stood up and flexed her muscles like Hulk Hogan. "These biceps are no joke."

Randall couldn't help but laugh as Ivey struck a faux boxing stance and mimed like she was in a tussle. "Because I'll hit that hoe with this left, right, right and left," Ivey said, right before holding both fists in the air like a newly crowned welterweight. "I'm the greatest!"

Randall took a drag of the blunt and shook his head while watching Ivey jog in a small circle, still with her hands up, going full Muhammad Ali. Randall grabbed her by the waist and kissed the back of her neck.

"Slow down champ, and catch this," Randall said, while passing the blunt to Ivey. "If there's one person you don't have to worry about, it's white girl Gretchen. I just think she is overly fascinated by my 'tales from the 'hood.' She always seems engrossed by what is pretty much commonplace occurrences."

After a long inhale, hold and exhale, Ivey's face turned serious.

"I love you, Randall. Be careful today, okay? I don't have any sets tonight, but I know how you feel about me coming out to these events."

Randall thought for a second before responding. It was true that Randall had persuaded Ivey to not attend events his was covering or otherwise involved in, but the reasons weren't all true.

While he told Ivey it was for her own safety - "Shit happens sometimes, baby, and I don't want you caught up" - was a familiar refrain he would tell Ivey, the real reason he didn't want her to come out was to protect Randall from himself.

Ivey was generally low-key jealous of women that tried to kick it to Randall, Randall would snap to the verge of outright hostility due to his jealous nature. That was an insecurity that Randall had yet to resolve.

"I love you as well, baby. And you know how I am. People know me, but people *know* you, and I have a hard time beating back your fans as is. Maybe I'm the one who needs to 'hulk up' in the face of all your admirers."

Randall then stood up and did his own version of Hulkamania, pointing to Ivey's '60s-era mannequin in the corner, and said, in a very Hoganesque way, "Well, you know, Mean Gene…"

Ivey almost died with laughter, choking out the smoke from her lungs while simultaneously trying to catch her breath. "Yeah, those pythons of yours will do some damage," Ivey said. "Come over here and finish this thing off so you're right for your day."

It was 1 p.m. when Marcus slid over to the front passenger seat after watching Randall exit Ivey's complex and looked on in mock shock, reflecting Randall's genuine surprise as he got into his car.

"What's good, champ? I thought you wouldn't mind giving your boy a lift," Marcus said. "And yo, you really need to be more careful about locking the doors to your whip; I would have waited outside, but your doors were unlocked."

Randall felt this mind imploding and exploding at the same time. Real-time reality seemed to bend and warp as he tried to rectify Marcus' appearance, and how he seemed to know so much about every detail of Randall's life. And knowing about the spare key was enough to send a bolt of ice down his spine. Worse, Randall couldn't shake the feeling that he met Marcus before, a very long time ago.

Randall already had to deal with Gretchen in a few, and he was starting to get fed up with Marcus' game of hide and seek.

"Man, what the fuck are you doing? You almost gave me a heart attack," Randall said as he started the car. "And I don't appreciate you just breaking into my shit like this. I know damn well I chirped the alarm."

Marcus smiled in a very slow and methodical manner, before giving up and simply laughing at Randall's tough-guy attempt.

"My man, stop that. You know you can trust me; we go way back, remember?" Marcus said in a very dismissive yet direct manner; one that was sort of airy but intense. "I like that heat, though; make sure hold some of that smoke for Gretchen. You know that white bitch is going to want to quiz you to death about the event tonight. Want me to come in with you?"

Randall startled himself when it dawned on him that he didn't even question how Marcus could have known about his meeting with Gretchen. But of course, Marcus knew. Marcus seemed to always know.

"I'm not really sweating Gretchen; she's just trying to cover her bases and protect her own ass, so I can respect that. But this fucking detective just will not stop harassing me about these two murders," Randall said while whipping his sedan through midday traffic. "This dude says I'm always around the murders, but shit, it seems like he's the one that's always around the killings. I have more of a reason to be at any of these events than he does, but he's trying to lean on me like I owe him something. He already pulled Ivey and I in for questioning, and I know he already contacted Gretchen and probably even the fucking publisher."

The sentiment caused an anger-fueled adrenaline spike; and as the steering wheel squealed under Randall's tightening grip and his left foot pushed toward the floor, Randall was slowly giving in to Marcus' passion for hate and understood it.

Marcus leaned back like a proud father, impressed with Randall's diatribe as his smile broadened.

"Well, that fuckin' flatfoot is going to be there tonight and will put a tail on you," Marcus said. "Not that he has a reason to suspect you of all people, but the lazy fuck wants you to do his work for him."

Randall interjected. "I don't know who is worse; these ass-backwards rappers propagating and disseminating the most based and fucked-up stereotypes of black people, or these fucking black cops who get their nut off by clipping brothers who are trying to get out of the game. Fuck 'em both."

A sense of freedom coursed through Randall's veins, the byproduct of finally realizing what Marcus has been trying to show him all along.

The clouds began clearing, but Randall still had two problems: Gretchen and Barron. His editor he could handle; but the detective proved to be more than a simple hindrance or some new cop just trying to feel his way around.

Randall felt threatened in a new way and knew his life would be better if Barron just went away.

"You deal with Gretchen; leave Barron to me," Marcus said after a moment of purposeful silence. "Don't let Gretchen talk you out of covering the event tonight. It's best if Barron sees you there anyway; that way, when the shit does pop off and if he believes his own eyes, then he will know you couldn't have possibly done anything."

Randall's mind, fixated on the meeting with Gretchen, payed little attention to Marcus' directive. The hate for Barron began to crystalize in Randall's mind, and he wondered exactly what it would take for him to be reassigned, or even better, tossed off the force altogether. Randall thought the chances were mighty slim that such an event would occur that would knock him off Randall's back and off the case.

"A number of things could happen to our buddy Detective Wilkinson," Marcus said. "He could get fucked up stepping out of his house, or while stepping into his car. Maybe he'll go for the old banana in the tailpipe routine. Don't worry about him; as a matter of fact, I hope he remains well enough to attend tonight's show."

Marcus threw back his head and released a full-throated laugh that must have originated deep within his bowels. All of Marcus' perfect teeth shimmered in the sunlight. Randall had nearly enough time to count the bicuspids before Marcus laugh disintegrated into a chuckle.

Randall found himself chuckling in unison with Marcus.

"Wouldn't that be some funny shit; homeboy hot on the trail and sprains his ankle chasing ghosts," Randall said. "Maybe he blows out a hamstring while the killer two-steps on him."

It dawned on Randall that the killing of Streaks and Bombay could be mere pixels in a much bigger picture that still hadn't quite come into focus.

Randall thought of all the similarities and differences between the two slain rappers. While they knew each other, Streaks and Bombay were from different parts of the city and ran with different crews that rarely interacted with one another.

And aside from each of the murdered emcees rapping about the same shit, Randall just couldn't conjure up another thread that connected the two rappers.

Gone now were Randall's typical depression-laden hangover from covering murders; the more Randall considered the events leading up to the demise of both rappers, he concluded that in the end, both rappers pretty much got what they deserved.

I mean, how many times can these rappers talk all that shit about drug dealing and throwing bullets around, before someone runs a credit check? Randall thought, no longer put off or offending himself with such thoughts. *Shit, you ask me, these motherfuckers had it coming; and besides, figuring out this whodunit is for the cops.*

Marcus had trouble stifling his smirk, putting a gloved hand to his mouth as he rode in the passenger seat next to Randall.

Marcus' face then exploded with a harrowing guffaw.

"Oh, you've *really* embraced this shit; that's it my man, let it out," Marcus said, in a way that was half cajole and half taunt. "I'm proud of you. It's about time to you've nutted up and saw these motherfuckers for what they really are - nothing but a bunch of sorry-ass cats who only got on because they could throw a few words together and talk shit that they can't back up.

"Like this cat tonight - what's his name again, Frostman? Now here is a motherfucker just asking to be made an example out of."

Frostman's whole persona was based on thing: pimping. Randall knew as a fact that Frostman fully stepped into that persona, as rumors had it that he actually had workers tricking out of a seedy strip-club in West Philly, and that he also operated a handful of other strip clubs on the southside.

That's not to mention the controlling interest Frostman supposedly has in the open-air strip of hooks on Wyalusing Avenue.

Randall was assigned to cover the L&I shutdown of one of those clubs, and Frostman and Randall have been on sour terms ever since. This beef was different, as Frostman, real name Derrick James McCoy, took real umbrage toward Randall over an issue totally unrelated to the music scene. For some reason, Frostman thought that since Randall was 'down' with the hip-hop scene, that Randall would go easy on his coverage of the shutdown.

That was a miscalculation, as Randall's piece not only hammered Frostman and the other owners for the series of code violations that led to the shutdown, but for being a black man operating such a tawdry business enterprise to begin with.

And although Randall couldn't outright print it, his article heavily alluded to Frostman's hand in the local pimp racket. To Randall, Frostman was little more than a sex trafficker who took things to a heightened personal level after the paper printed Randall's piece; he outright threatened to shoot Randall on sight due to the negative coverage.

Randall despised Frostman even more than the contempt he held for Streaks.

"Yeah, that's his name. And you know the main difference between Streaks and Bombay and this fuckin' Frostman? This guy's whole shit is corny; like showing up at the club with like five of his 'hoes, and with that fuckin' wide-brimmed leather hat. I should have tapped his chin at the club after he made that threat."

Marcus closed his eyes as a gapless smile unfurled from earlobe to earlobe; Randall indeed harbored a seething disdain for Frostman.

It was everything: the old-school Lincoln Continental he drove, how he treated women and his disrespect for the culture of hip-hop that triggered Randall. Frostman dripped and oozed every bit of the pimp hustle mixed with a dose of the drug game.

"But he's a small player on rap the scene, for real for-real. Most don't consider him as anything other than a gimmick, but I know I wouldn't give a shit if he fell off the stage and broke a leg or two."

Marcus sneered.

"Just a leg or two, huh? Well, we know he's going to perform tonight; maybe he'll have that chance," Marcus said in a very flat and serious tone. "That he threatened my man is not cool, though; he needs to bleed for that shit. What, he thinks he can threaten us, and we'll let that stand?"

Now Randall smirked as he thought of how satisfying it would be to pummel Frostman with his own two hands. Randall didn't take too kindly to the threat of gunplay from this cornball, but he also knew to never underestimate any man. As a result, Randall would always be on alert if he was in the same venue as Frostman.

As fate would have it, the two have rarely crossed paths since the day of that threat.

Marcus had a thought that intercepted his plans of accompanying Randall to the Liacouras Center later.

"Ayo, let me out right here," Marcus said, as Randall approached the red light at 24th and Fairmount. "I've got to dip and handle something. I'll catch up to you later."

As soon as Randall's Accord idled, Marcus hopped out and seemingly disappeared amongst the throng of people entering a corner bodega.

It was midday Wednesday by the time Randall whipped his Accord into his usual parking spot in the paper's garage. Randall entered the building through the back door, as was the usual entrance for workers who parked in the back.

On the way in, Randall bumped into Florence McDaniels, the associate copy desk editor. In her 30's, 'Flo' was more in line with Randall's line of thinking regarding news and coverage than her colleagues, an ideology that some in the newsroom whispered was the reason why she hadn't been promoted to full copy desk editor.

But as the associate, she attended many editorial meetings while also dodging most of the newsy shit when it hit the fan.

Flo and Randall bumped fists when they met.

"What's good, Flo? The desk treating you right?" Randall asked. "I hope they aren't giving you any shit for the lead headline you pitched. When I heard about it, I thought for sure they'd run it."

From time to time in plenary meetings, Flo would pitch the leading headline for the next day's paper, only to be shot down by her editorial superiors.

The paper's brass often thought Flo's headlines were a bit too aggressive, even by the paper's standards.

"You know how it is; always trying hold a sister down. But what's good with you? You're quite the talk of the newsroom nowadays."

The look on Randall's face was one of surprise blended with a healthy amount of apprehension.

"Word? I hope the talk has been of the 'Randall is the shit' variety?"

Flo laughed. "Nah, just dealing with the copy desk fitting your article, and the growing amount of attention being paid to your stories by those on the outside."

"One the outside?" Randall asked, trying to mask the growing alarm in his voice. "Like who?"

Flo's face turned dark as she darted eyes around the newsroom before answering.

"The police have been calling and stopping by, Randall. From what I gather, they are still trying to pump Gretchen for your contacts and making her account for how you manage to be so much on top of these recent killings."

Flo moved in closer, talking in that tone that registered just above a whisper but low enough for no one else to hear her. "And on the low, some detective was here earlier, and met with Gretchen for two hours. Closed door jawn."

Randall blinked, and stood motionless. He knew exactly who it was.

"Detective Barron Wilkinson," Randall said, with an acute edge in his voice. "This fucking cop is trying to build his case off of my hard work, and he even drug Ivey and I down to the Roundhouse for statements and whatnot Monday night. I don't know what dude thinks, but he creeps me the hell out."

Flo nodded. Even though the paper had an unofficial comply agreement with the police department, journalists were very leery of providing police with too much information. After all, reporter immunity only went so far.

Both Flo and Randall knew of several reporters who were attacked, and three even killed, after they cooperated with the police.

"Well, at least you know what time it is," Flo said. "Stay strong, soldier."

As Randall watched Flo flash the two-finger "peace" sign and glide down the walkway on the far side of the newsroom, he felt a growing anger. A pure fire directed at Barron. *This motherfucker is trying to get me fired. If Gretchen didn't fold in front of him, then she is surely going to ask me to divulge a source. But there is no fuckin' source. I just happen to be the right person in the wrong place at the right time.*

When Randall arrived at his desk, he had several voicemails waiting for him, along with a bright-yellow sticky-note plastered to the center of his computer monitor.

"My office. ASAP." Read the note, in Gretchen's handwriting.

Fuck me. She just won't let up.

Taking a deep and slow breath, Randall gathered his notebook, pen and iPhone and started for Gretchen's office.

"Here I am," Randall said, after knocking on the open office door. "What's up?"

Gretchen seemed more pale than usual, and slightly unkempt, as if she had a long morning, if not a longer night.

"Randall, close the door, and after you do, answer me this one question, please: what the FUCK is going on?"

Randall knew he was in deep. That type of tone is usually reserved for those at the very end of their tenure at the paper.

Randall shot her a quizzical look after shutting the door. "Gretchen, what are you talking about?"

"You know very well what I'm talking about, so don't play those games with me. Fucking homicide has been calling here for the last two days about these murders, murders you just so happened to be on the scene for. They want to know just how you have managed to have such first-hand knowledge of these incidents, like you are always around when shit happens."

Randall looked Gretchen dead in the face and answered in kind.

"Gretchen, back up for one second. This isn't the first time the police have approached us when they couldn't solve some crime on their own. They are lazy, just like those goddamned broadcast news reporters with their long-throw lenses," Randall said while giving off a sharp vibe that Gretchen undoubtedly received.

"And I know it's mainly Detective Barron Wilkinson who is giving you a hard time. He's the same cop that dragged Ivey and I down for questioning Monday night. Point-blank: I have no connections nor insider information about these murders.

"I know less than the cops do. And even if I did have a confidential source, I certainly wouldn't give him up to Barron. Snitches get stitched up; you know how it goes."

Gretchen clearly was not in the mood for any of that shit.

"Randall, this is different than keeping a confidential source. You know when you have a CS, you should check with me first regarding the individual's identity, for legal clearinghouse purposes. That way, I can vet the source and vouch for you. You know this," Gretchen said, her voice escalating with every consonant. "I met for two hours with this fucking detective. I told him over and over that I didn't know anything about your contacts, and he said could attempt to get more information by subpoena; a fucking subpoena, Randall.

"Even then, I argued that there probably isn't any more to your story than what was printed, and reminded him that as reporters, we are covered by the state's Privacy Protection Act. But the problem for you and me, Randall, is that I believe there is a contact of some sort, and you're holding out on me," Gretchen added, now standing a mere three feet from Randall. It was apparent that all five feet, three inches and 120 pounds of Gretchen wanted to go nose-to-nose with Randall on this issue. "I know all about protecting a source, so don't run that con on me.

"So, tell me here and now, right here and right now: do you know something about these murders that you're not telling me or the cops? I'm only going to ask this one time, and your answer is your answer."

As she waited for Randall's response, Gretchen folded her arms high on her chest and cocked her head slightly to left, almost as if she was ready to square off in a breakdancing battle.

Randall had the damnedest thought of breaking out in a floor routine, complete with a windmill.

Randall's second thought had to do with the sheer audacity of this chick coming at him with that tone. Editor or not.

"And I'm only going to say this once and once only: I. Do. Not. Have. Any. Fucking. Contacts. That's it. How would I?" Randall said after taking a deliberately long minute to ponder his answer. "Do I look like I run with the types that would have something to do with these murders? How long have you known me, Gretchen? You know I always give you information first. But there is simply nothing to give you."

Randall found that his voice was now rising as well, meeting Gretchen's decibel level. Several staffers walking by took a moment to peer through the glass of Gretchen's office, no doubt wanting to catch the yelling match.

"This detective has you shook, especially if you're coming at me like this," Randall added, now striking a much more offensive tone. "Maybe we should instead focus on this bullshit 'hip-hop cop' and find out why he's solely interested in these cases. I've done my own research on him. Did you know that he was from the homicide unit in New York and volunteered to dime out rap artists that had one foot in the streets and the other in the studio? Do you know he was implicated in the murder of a rapper in Queens before coming here? You're coming at me, but trust me, you don't know this detective's full story."

Gretchen seemed genuinely surprised by this information. She unfolded her arms, stepped back and sat down, taking a moment to process what Randall just revealed.

"How did you find this out? I don't even think our Roundhouse reporters knew this. And anyway, what does that have to do with anything? You know like we all do that certain cops have beats, especially detectives. Some work cases about the mob and organized crime only, and some focus on murders by region," Gretchen said, in a way that was an effort to calm both her and Randall and to take some of the steam out of the conversation. "Just like we have certain writers that cover crime only, and some that cover features; it just so happens that you cover both.

"Randall, I'm only looking out for you - and the paper."

Randall knew the first part of Gretchen's statement was pure bullshit, but the second part, about looking out for the paper, was a fact.

Randall survived long enough in the newspaper game to know that when it comes right down it, the paper will protect itself, and will ultimately leave writers hanging out to try.

Randall's mind skipped back to that time he was sued by a political kingmaker over a typo, of all things.

The paper's publisher and general manager wanted Randall to take full ownership of the error, although in the end, it was discovered that an opinion page editor, with an axe to grind against the operative, doctored the actual piece that landed Randall in hot water - and with a seat in front of the lawyer for said kingmaker.

Randall had no legal representation during that hearing, and he hasn't forgiven the paper since. Randall had a hard moving on from that incident.

Without a doubt, it's all about the paper, Randall thought.

"Gretchen, I wouldn't try to jam you up on anything. But if you just look at this objectively, it's an easy add. I cover the hip-hop scene, and if something happened at one of the bigger shows, then of course I'm going to be there. And it only makes some sort of sense that the police would want to question me about it. And if they think I'm holding out - which, again, I am not - then of course at that point they would put the clamps on my editor, who in turn would apply downward pressure on me to give up the goods," Randall said. "Now, I don't know why this detective had such a hard-on for me, but I can only tell you what I know and what I think."

Randall believed that this conversation would end in a stalemate, and also knew it would linger. Still, Randall had work to do: filing some random human-interest story before prepping coverage for the show later that evening.

"Randall, I told you I would only ask you once, and you gave me your answer. I won't ask you again," Gretchen said in a way that sounded like half promise and half warning. "So, what do you have planned for tonight?"

"Photo has been assigned," Randall said. "Potsie shouldn't bitch too much about this assignment."

Pylma "Potsie" Dotson was the lead night-side photographer, and on this night, he was the only photographer available, at any rate. "I don't think he'll be able to stay for the entire event, because as you know his priority is spot crime coverage.

"Otherwise, I plan on getting there a bit early as usual and will have 20 inches for you in time for Thursday's paper."

Gretchen nodded.

"It's at Liacouras, right? That should be fine. Remember, drop-dead is 11:30 pm. I'll make sure the copy desk pushes this for Thursday, as long as Potsie sends over the images in time; but don't be salty if it's held until Friday," Gretchen said. "Oh, and just to let you know, Detective Wilkinson said he was going to attend this concert as well. He seems to think he could find out more about those murders by surveying the crowd and talking to a few people."

"I'll be sure to say hello when I see him," Randall said, his words leaking with sarcasm. "Him and I, we're homies now, ya know."

"See you tomorrow afternoon, Randall," Gretchen retorted. "You know, you're lucky you are as good as you think you are."

Fucking sakes; these meetings with Gretchen are turning into sparring matches, Randall thought as he returned to his desk.

Randall quickly filed his piece on the opening of a new medical center on Haverford Avenue, and since he had time, he decided to call Ivey and see if she was open for him popping through.

* * * * *

CAPTAIN Carmichael Fleming was not in a good mood.

He sat staring at the nondescript wall clock and watched the hour hand tick to five, which led to a faint yet distinct minute-long klaxon that served as an unofficial alarm for shift change.

Carmichael knew that Barron would be checking in with him before joining the detail at the Liacouras Center, but wanted to make it crystal clear to his lone-wolf detective that this may very well be the *last* time he checked in.

Especially after Cammie's phone call with Police Commissioner Ryan Miller.

Commissioner Miller, himself a lifelong Philadelphian who rose up through the ranks and hired by the mayor just a year before these recent murders, made anti-crime his most hirable selling point. He dazzled that mayor with his plans and promises to root out inner-city murders - starting with the aggressive patrols of known gathering spots and locales.

The commissioner performed the same magic trick in front of City Council members when it was their turn to vet and eventually affirm the mayor's latest police chief.

Although fairly new, Commissioner Miller was furious that these murders occurred on *his* watch, and he relayed those feelings to his captain in a tense phone call.

"Cammie, the Mayor is on my ass about these murders. City Council is on HIS ass about doing something about it," the commissioner said during the phone call that concluded just a few minutes prior.

"Council wants answers, the Mayor wants answers, and I want answers. Tell me where things stand, and I then I will tell you where *you* stand."

Cammie knew all too well what that meant.

"Sir, my men and I are doing the best we can, given the circumstances. We have had some information trickling in, and we are running down every lead. It has just been difficult in securing information from less-than-helpful neighbors and would-be witnesses," Cammie said, flinching at the sound of his own apologetic voice. "We have stills and video surveillance of the second murder scene provided by nearby business cameras, and we are working now to identify certain individuals.

"Otherwise, we have also dedicated extra manpower toward solving these killings."

"That sounds a lot like the shit I used to tell my captain," Ryan said, wholly unimpressed with Cammie's breakdown. "In other words, if a fly took a shit in a thimble, you'd have less than that to go on. What the hell has Detective Wilkinson been doing? You had full autonomy to bring him in and add him to your team, which pissed off a number of rank-and-file locals who, by the way, thought there were better positioned to take the lead on these rap murders.

"And that's not even talking about the protests started by the neighborhood Police Advisory Commissions, who have now interrupted Council's proceedings for the third straight session. So this is on you, Cammie. What is your prized detective doing about this?"

"Sir, Barron is working on these cases, and he actually thinks he's close to solving them. He is going to the Liacouras Center tonight. He is also grilling some reporter, trying to wring more information out of him.

"Seems this reporter, Randall Jenkins, actually covers these sorts of hip-hop shows, and happened to be there or around the last two murders," Cammie said. "Barron believes he's more attached to the situation than he is letting on to be."

Ryan was familiar with Randall through the reporter's coverage of his ascension. The commissioner considered Randall to be a media friend to the police, for whatever that was worth. The commissioner didn't want to sour that relationship, but he also knew solving these murders were of paramount importance; it became clear that investigators would have to ruffle a few feathers to get the information they needed.

"I know Randall; good people. But if you really feel he is holding back, then go harder. But remember, he has rights too, and the paper wouldn't like it if we played rough with one of their reporters, especially one who covers some of our work," Ryan said. "But Cammie, let me warn you: the success or failure of these investigations will ultimately fall on me, then you.

"The Mayor will expect his own pint of blood if these murders continue to go unsolved; and I would be obliged to make sure he got it."

Cammie wiped his brow after disconnecting with his superior, and his sour disposition wasn't lost on Barron when he entered his captain's office.

"Cammie, you wanted to see me?"

"Shut the door and sit down, Wilkinson," Cammie said. "The Commissioner just tore me a new asshole over your so-far fruitless investigation.

"So, I'm going to tell you as the Commissioner told me: it's our asses on the line if we – if *you* - cannot come up with the killer. And before I get all the blame, you can be sure stories will be written about how the 'heralded New York detective who couldn't hack it in Philly was let go.'"

The threat to Barron was real and hit home in nearly a physical way. Feeling winded but still confident that he was on the right track, Barron sat down and laid it out for his captain.

"Look Cammie, I know it may seem like there's little headway being made, but I know I can catch this guy; just let me finish this thing out," Barron said. "The investigation, along with my own sense, tells me that this reporter knows more than he's letting on. I met with his editor earlier today, and she backed him up for the most part. But when I asked about how he was in general, she said something very interesting. It may be something, or nothing at all."

Cammie sighed and sat back in his chair.

Okay; let's have it."

"Well, she said that for the last few months, Randall just hasn't seemed like himself. She thought maybe it was because he was becoming burnt out," Barron said. "She thought of trimming back his workload, but he always wanted go to extra-hard at every story. She also said that Randall's writing was slipping a bit too."

Cammie was not impressed.

"Fascinating. Not please tell me exactly what the fuck all of that has to do with anything," Cammie said, staring a hole directly through Barron's face.

"Like I said, it probably means nothing. I just have a strong hunch about this guy, that he knows more than he says does, and he might be close to cracking. And I want to ask him some more questions after tonight's concert," Barron said. "He's covering the event for the paper, so he'll be in my sights for most of the night.

"One way or the other, after tonight, I shouldn't have any more use for Mr. Jenkins."

Cammie still wasn't convinced, bur he decided to extend Barron's rope just a bit longer.

"Okay, detective, then you have tonight - plus one week - to either solve this particular string of murders or produce a prime suspect.

"And as far as putting the pinch on this reporter, just remember that the newspaper is known to be particularly sensitive about law enforcement leaning on it is staff, and the paper's owners have become quite fuckin' litigious over it," Cammie went on. "Unless you want to add being sued to your growing list of accomplishments, I'd say be careful on how you approach him from now on. Do what you have to do but do it within the law - and within ten days."

Chapter Eight

DETECTIVE Barron Wilkinson knew what time it was, or more precisely, now knew how much time he had. The captain gave him ten days to make substantial headway into solving these two murders, which bore hallmarks consistent with them being committed by a lone operator; the same operator.

Retreating to his office, Barron focused on all of the facts, evidence and data connected to and gathered on these two murders, which Barron concluded were more interconnected than initially thought.

There was the timing of each murder, with each occurring less than 30 minutes after the artist finished performing; the killer apparently used no weapons at all in dispatching the slain rappers, meaning the killer most likely had some sort of personal grudge; and the killer was somehow able to overpower his victims, probably through the element of surprise.

Barron couldn't ascertain if the victims knew or recognized their killer. That's where he believed Randall fit in. After all, and with all things considered, who had more knowledge of the area's rappers and the shit they're involved in than Randall?

Barron knew from his days in New York that what is printed in the papers hardly ever told the full story, and Barron was certain that Randall knew more than what he was telling the public and investigators.

Barron just couldn't let go of that nagging feeling that gnawed at his gut, screaming at him about Randall.

Not a believer in coincidence and for a long time understanding that $1 + 1 = 2$, Barron knew, but could not yet prove, that Randall was aware of the killer's identity.

Still, as elusive as the killer has turned out to be, Barron wasn't going to take any chances tonight.

Barron called Lieutenant Frank Tolliver. The lieutenant served as the nightside command for the district and was responsible for coordinating police coverage for the event at the center.

"This is Lt. Tolliver."

"Frank, this is Wilkinson. Just wanted to check in with you about tonight and request a few extra men to guard the nearby subway stations and parking lots.," Barron said. "Maybe about a dozen or so men."

"Detective, we already have five officers and three units assigned to tonight's event, and we've coordinated with Temple University Police on providing eyes-and-ears support and secondary backup," the lieutenant said. "We also have two men inside, both in plainclothes. Other than that, I cannot promise you any more manpower. We are already stretched thin as it is."

"That will have to do," Barron said, thankful for any extra men he could get. "I think tonight we get closer to our man."

*****

IVEY anxiously waited for Randall and peeped out her window, relieved to see Randall pull into the parking lot.

Well, at least he survived his showdown with Gretchen," Ivey thought to herself, watching Randall gather himself before making his way up to her unit.

Although he had a key, it was Randall's custom to ring Ivey's bell and wait for her to answer.

At the chime, Ivey, dressed in a matching bra and bottom loungewear that featured a repeating print of various historical turntables, lit the blunt she just prepared and answered the door.

"Oh, a handsome stranger. You lost, sugar? I know you're not looking for me," Ivey said, taking a dramatic step back and clutching her throat in a mock love-swept manner. "I declare, what am I to do with you but smoke this here finely rolled blunt and gaze upon yo' figure."

"Ah, darlin', ain't you just about the prettiest lil' concrete daisy this asphalt cowpoke has ever laid eyes on," Randall said, right in step with Ivey's play. "A man sure could make himself a home here; now come closer, let this 'rassler take a good gander upon ya."

Ivey laughed and jumped in Randall's arms, nearly giving him an unintentional shotgun with the blunt.

"I'm glad you made it through the meeting with Gretchen, baby; I had a bad vibe all day about how things were going to go."

"So, everything is everything?"

Randall gave Ivey a tight squeeze before letting her body slide down his. Randall always took whatever moment he could to enjoy Ivey's curves. Randall then took off his Timberlands before taking the blunt from Ivey.

"It was her usual shit. She came at me really husky because detective Wilkinson paid her an unannounced, two-hour visit," Randall said. "She was under the impression - or, I should say, Barron gave her the impression - that I was holding out on both her and the police department. No doubt about it, Barron is one grimy cat. But otherwise, I killed that noise with Gretchen, and all attention turned towards tonight's event."

"That damn detective is surely giving everyone a headache," Ivey said between puffs of the blunt Randall had just handed her. "The cops can't come up with a lead, but they can come up with all these wild theories that you know something. Barron should be ashamed of himself; doesn't he know that these types of moves can fuck up a black man's livelihood?"

Randall loved it when Ivey became righteously indignant on his behalf. Randall always felt as though he had an armed angel on his shoulder whenever Ivey stood up for him.

"Indeed. And of course, I expect to see him tonight. He all but told Gretchen he'd be there."

Ivey paused a moment, took yet another pull and passed the blunt back to Randall before finally nodding her head in agreement.

"Baby, you know I never interfere with your work; but I worry about you, and I wouldn't mind if you never covered these events again. Besides, you already know who the illest DJ in the city is," Ivey said with a small curl to the side of her lips while referring to the DJ battle that was part of the night's showcase. "But seriously, I don't think anyone would be too mad at you for stepping back from all this shit; and if they did get salty about it, fuck 'em anyway.

"Besides, that would give you more time to focus on your gig - and me."

When Randall looked up at Ivey's face, he could tell from her eyes that she was speaking from the soul.

What she didn't say but implied through the undertone in her voice was that this would also take Randall out of the eye of the storm that were these murders and the general angst and overall bullshit that came with covering local hip-hop. Randall didn't *have* to attend every event to show his support for the culture.

And Randall, always a proponent of self-preservation, had to agree with Ivey. *Shit, if it weren't for tonight's assignment, I wouldn't even bother going,* Randall thought.

"Who can resist those eyes of yours? Although it's a shame; I won't be able to cast my vote for the best deejay in Philly."

As Randall tried in vain to dip the oncoming right hook from Ivey, she managed to punch Randall hard on the arm, frogging up his bicep. "Don't make me hurt you, Randall. Those plaques didn't hang themselves, you know."

Across town and attending as another sort of spectator altogether, Detective Barron Wilkinson also prepped for the night's event.

Dressed in a black turtleneck, dark denim jeans and a camel-colored leather jacket, Barron's attire would allow him to easily and anonymously blend into the crowd. After lacing up a pair of black-on-white Nike Air Max trainers, Barron gave himself the once-over in the body-length mirror in his apartment.

Satisfied, the detective tucked the flap of his gold detective shield into the left side of the waist of his jeans and stuffed his police-issue Glock into the small of his back. He then strapped a baby .32 revolver and its custom low-profile holster to the area of shin right above the ankle. Barron came to appreciate the usefulness of having a little backup, never knowing how these sorts of operations will play out.

After glancing down at his Tag Heuer Carrera and lighting a Newport, Barron closed his eyes and thought of the tactical plan he devised for tonight while simultaneously chasing around the facts of these murders in his mind.

Barron also thought of the high stakes involved with tonight's operation. If he wasn't able to link the facts together with more tangible evidence, Barron knew he would have to ostensibly start the investigation over from the top. He could feel the seconds thundering by, all the while replaying Cammie's threat in his mind.

This investigation could very well make my career or end it, Barron thought, taking a long pull of his cigarette. *I know that fuckin' reporter knows more than what he told me and his editor.*

If anything, Barron was keenly aware of the thin ice upon which he was now skating, and that one more fuck up, one more swing-and-miss, and he could very well be packing his desk for the second time in as many years.

That sent a chill down Barron's spine, as did another thought.

Could I be all wrong about Randall, though? Can it really be someone else who has nothing to do with Randall, and I've been chasing down the wrong man all this time?

That consideration sent Barron to his spare bedroom.

Once inside the bedroom, Barron pushed an empty, rickety bookshelf a few feet to the left, unveiling a door to a once-forgotten storage room. Barron unlocked the door and entered.

Once inside, Barron pulled the cord to the bald lightbulb hanging three feet above his head. After the reassuring click, the bulb threw 360 degrees of raw light throughout the small space.

The first thing Barron did when he discovered the unadvertised room was to convert it to his liking;

the space now served as Barron's sanctuary and stash spot.

In it, Barron kept an assortment of items that singularly would have him thrown off the force and most likely indicted. Half the items Barron couldn't reasonably explain away to his superiors, and the other half of his lot would be considered straight-up illegal, in anyone's hands.

Barron had several weapons he lifted from criminals and evidence lockers in New York and Philadelphia; to the left, trays filled with of authentic and counterfeit drugs and pills, including marijuana, ecstasy, Oxytocin, cocaine and heroin.

Barron meticulously tended to his stash, running his fingers across the illicit goods like a jeweler mesmerized by a batch of asscher cut diamonds.

Barron had dozens of clear cellophane baggies filled with coke and withdrew one, along with a tenth of a gram of high-grade marijuana he seized from a Dominican runner in Port Richmond.

While Barron didn't disturb it, he kept his most coveted items in a safe at the back of the small room.

Barron's spared no expense for the special-edition Rhino-CD3022 safe and paid quite the sum to have it installed but deemed it an occupational must-have.

Barron dashed the light and exited the small room, locking the door behind him. He then pushed the bookcase back to its former position before heading to the kitchen.

There, Barron separated his goods into piles to whip up his most favorite form of escapism: smoking the potent marijuana which he laced with some of the Dominicans' coke.

After putting together his Garcia y Vega blunt, Barron lit it and could feel the intoxicating vapor enveloping his mind as he thought deeper about his tenuous position.

Taking another long draw, Barron picked up his thoughts regarding the possibility of Randall being an innocent reporter just caught up in this latest drama. After all, was it that weird that Randall would happen to be at the scene of these two murders? There could have been literally hundreds of people that attended both events.

I'm going to need more than my gut feelings to try to pin a murder rap on some fucking reporter, Barron all but concluded, facing the cold reality that he has not developed a secondary suspect nor alternate theory. Barron knew that he painted himself into a tight corner by tossing all of his eggs into the Randall basket. But the detective also figured he had a few more angles he could pursue to get to the bottom of these cases. *It's not too late to switch gears; if tonight doesn't pan out, I know just the next route to take.*

Barron's eyes began to burn and tear as the toxic fumes of the laced weed began to form a thick, strange haze that seemed to hover in midair. Barron could feel his head beginning to float as he dragged the blunt down to the burnt end.

Initially off-balance, Baron regained his equilibrium as he rose from his couch and headed back to the kitchen.

Barron ran the spigot and rubbed the bunt end between his fingers as the warm water washed the remnants of the proof of his high down the drain. He then washed his hands to his elbows for five minutes, before meticulously cleaning his nails. Barron took extreme precautions to cleanse himself of any contraband particulates. *You never know,* Barron thought.

Still high off the laced marijuana, Barron returned to the living room and looked over the space to make sure he didn't leave any hint of his prior activities. While visitors were few, Barron knew he couldn't stop his superiors from unexpectantly popping over.

After one last look in the mirror, Barron then sent a text to Lieutenant Toliver, and made hie way to the Liacouras center.

Barron met Frank's detail and campus police at Temple's Campus Safety Services offices, only a three-block distance from the Liacouras Center.

Frank was seated behind TUP's captain's desk and addressing the five Philly cops and the TUP officers when Barron entered. Temple's police sergeant had left the meeting prior to Barron's arrival, as he was responsible for the overall planning on Temple's side and already briefed his men.

"Detective, I was just explaining to the full team the nature of tonight's operation, beyond providing general security for the attendees and surrounding businesses and residents," Frank said. "But perhaps you could explain it in more detail to them. But keep in mind that on Temple's side, they have more experience than we do in dealing with events here at the center."

Barron took that as a cue to go soft on the Temple officers, and to make sure they had an appreciable part of the action. The Roundhouse has fielded its share of complaints from transit and university police department heads who felt city police often didn't consider other law enforcement officers as 'real' cops.

"Gentlemen, I appreciate your time and willingness to act as eyes and ears," Barron said. "As you know, there have been two murders at two recent hip-hop events, and I want to make sure a third does not happen tonight.

"The murderer may or may not try to strike tonight; he may or may not attend," Barron continued, lightly treading on the fact that he has no suspect composite and no other discerning physical trait to go on. "Your team will provide the EAE, but I will be circulating through the crowd and backstage to check on things. I plan on being visible without being seen."

"Who and what are you looking for?" One of the Temple officers asked.

"I'm not too sure, not yet; but I'll let you know as soon as I do," Barron responded. "But what I do know is that tonight's show represents the biggest and most hyped underground rap show of the year, and if our man is going to do anything at all, such as looking for his next victim, he is going to do it tonight. Just keep an eye out for anything that looks even remotely out of place."

A light grumble emerged from the group before Frank sharply tapped his Zippo lighter against the desk.

"Listen up: we've coordinated with SEPTA police to double the officers at the Cecil B. Moore and Susquehanna-Dauphin subway stations, and we have a plan for a coordinated presence regarding surface transit at the bus stops in the immediate area surrounding the center; most of you will be assigned to that coverage," Frank said. "Usual security and metal detectors at the door; no K-9's. Detective Wilkinson here and I will be responsible for limited-access areas, such as the loading dock, entertainment-only entrances and bathrooms, greenroom and of course, the stage."

Barron rolled his eyes. *That sort of loud coverage may scare off the killer, if he bothers to show up tonight,* Barron thought. Barron knew it was generally the sound course of action have a solid mix of uniformed and plain-clothed officers for this type of event, but for his purposes, Barron Began to feel the opportunity slip away of either identifying or coming close to identifying the killer.

For the detective, there was just no way that the killer would make an attempt for his third victim at such a publicized, and well-guarded, event.

Nonetheless, Barron issued his final orders and head's-up to the assembled officers, and made his way to the Liacouras Center, with its marquee seemingly shining brighter than usual. It threw a kaleidoscope of light all the way across Broad Street.

Once inside the center, Barron made his way to the off-limits stage and green room areas. It struck him how eerily similar this layout was to that of Sidewalk Soco, the scene of the second murder. Even the bathroom, situated off-center and down a short flight of steps, bore an uncanny resemblance to Soco's layout.

Barron had macabre thought that if the murderer did strike tonight, he would have no problems maneuvering around this space.

It was now an hour and half before the curtain raised on the show, and just about the time Barron finished double-checking the emergency exits nearest the sage, Randall was kissing Ivey as he, too, was preparing to hop in his Accord and make his way to the center.

But before he left, Randall had a strange feeling, and turned back toward Ivey.

"Baby, I don't know why, but I am having a real strange vibe about tonight's show. Not that any shit will pop off, but something feels unsettled. I know you weren't actually planning to go, but if you were -

please don't."

Ivey almost laughed out loud, but instead she coughed out a lung-full of marijuana smoke.

"Randall, look at me. Does it look like I'm about to get dressed and go all the way to the Liacouras Center just for Frostman's show and to see some deejays, well, deejay? You're going find me just as you leave me now, in my bra and panties, smoking, waiting for you.

"But I find it loving and also a bit scary that you don't want me to show up tonight. You better not have some bitch on the side."

Randall smiled, before hugging Ivey.

"Nah baby, of course nothing like that. It's just that I don't want you to worry so much about me that you can't fight the compulsion to come down and save me. You are my superwoman, but I want you to have the night off."

Doing such a thing wasn't beyond Ivey. There have been previous events where Ivey, either out of pure jealousy, caring for Randall's safety, or some combination of the two, would find herself, unannounced, at an event that Randall as judging or merely attending. Randall never had an issue when Ivey showed up; to him, it was like a beautiful apparition unfolding before his very eyes whenever he did see Ivey making her way towards him.

When Randall made it to his sedan, his mind was fully focused on strictly attending this event, getting the results, and banging out a quickie report.

Randall's mind couldn't possibly have on his mind his backseat passenger, Marcus.

Chapter Nine

RANDALL and Marcus drove for some time before Marcus broke the silence by moving to the front passenger seat. Marcus had no problem scooting up and over the Accord's middle armrest before alighting to the seat, not unlike a loose down feather settling on a weathered comforter.

Marcus smiled, and Randall watched in amazement as Marcus' grin widened, and widened still. In what felt like slow-motion unfolding at 45 miles per hour, Randall stared in half horror and half bewilderment as Marcus' lips receded, displaying inhumanly perfect teeth, including the immaculate diamond-encrusted front tooth. Incredibly, Marcus' scar didn't budge.

"So, Randall, how do you want to do it?"

"Do what," Randall, replied, somehow knowing exactly what Marcus was referring to.

"Man, you crack me up," Marcus said. "I especially like the nice touch of telling your lady to not show up tonight. One less eyewitness. Especially one as close to you as Ivey is; that could possibly fuck up all your plans.

"And we can't have anyone, or anything, fucking up our plans."

Randall shuddered as he felt shards of ice shoot through his veins, coupled with an odd rush of adrenalin. It was an almost unbearable feeling, but the painful sensation was soon replaced by a surge of warmth, then with straight heat.

"And what plans are those," Randall retorted in the most dead-ass serious tone he could muster. "You know, you know talk too much; *too* fucking much. I have put up with your bullshit and fucking mind tricks since the day you walked into the cafe, and I let a lot of shit slide."

Randall then pulled over at the corner of Broad and Master Street, a few blocks from the center.

"And I don't take kindly to you being all up in my private business, with me and my lady and me and my gig," Randall continued, now fully squared with Marcus in the tightening confines of the Accord. "You might as well get the fuck out right here and make your own way to the center. I don't want to fucking see you again, and I *better* not see you again."

Marcus seemed generally struck by Randall's tone and stance. Before slowly cocking his head to the left and then right, Marcus appeared to get himself ready to exit the Accord.

But before stepping out, Marcus turned to Randall, and looked him dead in the eye.

"You know what? This is close enough for me; I can walk from here," Marcus said in a light and breezy voice that sounded quite non-confrontational and entirely out of place. "But before I do, can you hand me my gloves out of the glove compartment?"

Randall, almost in a blind rage due to Marcus' flippant reaction to his heat, hurriedly opened the glove compartment and tossed the pair black leather gloves at Marcus. Randall couldn't remember exactly how he got them or how they wound up in his glove compartment. Randall just always knew they were there and somehow belonged there.

No more, however, as Randall watched Marcus put them on.

"Snug fit, as ever," Marcus said. "Oh, and before I go, I just want to know how you are going explain why and how you murdered Streaks and Levi. I don't think what you told the cops is going to stick, especially for Barron. Shit, I bet he's already at the center just waiting for you to show up to bang you for those two killings.

"So, if I were you, I would go over my alibi one or two more times, before running that bullshit by the investigators again. What a shame. Better use that pen game of yours to come up with some surefire copy to grease your ass out of this bit of drama."

Marcus face and words now dripped with a sense of damning condescension, the kind usually dispensed by a chess *Grand Maistre* to an easily dispatched and otherwise hapless neophyte.

Randall felt a vise of pressure pressing against his temples. Indeed, he felt cornered by Marcus' gambit, and Randall's response was akin to that of a cornered tiger with hunger pangs.

"Oh yeah? Fuck you, Marcus. How do I know you didn't kill those two motherfuckers? Shit, as far as I know and can remember, you were always conveniently absent at the time when both these rappers where killed. Everybody knows where I was, but no one knows where you were.

"You want to threaten me? Suppose when that detective comes around again, I tell him a little bit more about you, and how these murders began only after you got here.

"Now, like I said, get the fuck out, and take your gloves and threats with you."

Marcus simply nodded.

"Well, I guess it all depends on who gets to Barron first," Marcus said. "But I'm sure he's going to have his hand's full tonight."

Randall grew infuriated as Marcus sat there, seemingly taunting him, daring Randall to follow through on his boisterous front.

After giving Marcus a very hard stare that lasted a very long three seconds, Randall got out of his Accord with every intention of airing it all out with Marcus, right then and there.

As Randall made his way around the front of his car, Marcus seemed to be a step ahead, already standing on the curb waiting for him.

Fuck this, and fuck him, Randall steamed to himself as he approached the altogether nonchalant Marcus.

"What now, tough guy? You sure you want to get fucked up, right here on the spot?" Marcus said in a tone that was new and eerie to Randall. But Randall wasn't about to let Marcus' posture dissuade him from getting right in Marcus' chest. "I brought that shit out in you, and I can beat the rest of it out of your bitch ass, right fuckin' now."

Randall snapped.

Randall's mouth filled with the taste of hot blood, a side effect of the rush of adrenaline and feral rage now overtaking his senses.

In a flash, Randall gripped Marcus by either side of his leather hipster jacket, wrapping the buttery soft cowhide between the fingers of his clinched and balled fists. In a feat of strength and in one fluid motion, Randall pushed Marcus, hard, up against the black arrow-topped fencing of an outdoor parking garage.

Breathing hard and close enough to kiss Marcus, Randall seethed out an unmistakable insult followed by a series of clear reinforcements.

"The only pussy here is you," Randall whispered in Marcus' ear. *And that's the last mistake you'll make.*

Releasing his grip on Marcus' leather jacket, Randall, using a short but powerful motion, slapped Marcus hard enough to break his jaw. The stinging sensation in Randall's hand only further enraged Randall, now hysterical with anger and consumed with an acute sense of retributive viciousness.

Randall then gave Marcus two very stiff and hooking body shots, before landing a tight left cross that sent Marcus stumbling to the concrete.

Randall, singularly minded on destroying Marcus and blinded by a lifetime of pent-up angst that began with being mercilessly bullied in grade school, put Marcus in a rear chokehold before dragging him back to the fence.

"Who's the pussy now?" Randall hissed in Marcus' ear. *I am going to kill this motherfucker right now.*

Randall flashed on all the times he was picked on in school. Taunted for being poor. Ridiculed for not fitting in. For being slight in size and stature. For not being cool. For not having a girlfriend. Or any friends. Or a father. Or an attentive mother.

Randall clenched his eyes hard enough to cause the capillaries in his eyes to burst and leak blood.

Randall's mind skated across the various and numerous lowlight moments in his life, humiliating instances where he was left powerless to react; times when Randall would get jumped and would run home from the playground. Times when there was no one to defend him, no one to stop the pain.

Randall felt an electrifying spasm of joy surge through his body as he transferred all that pain to Marcus. But just before what Randall thought was sure to be Marcus' last breath, he released his chokehold.

For an instant, Randall thought that he really did kill Marcus, as he watched Marcus slump to the ground.

Aghast, Randall took a step backward and toward the corner, bloodshot eyes bulging.

What am I doing?

The disturbance grabbed the attention of several onlookers passing by, including a pair of TUP officers.

After a brief discussion and exchanging chatter on a shoulder-holstered radio, one of the officers made his way to the parked Accord while the other approached Randall.

"Everything okay, sir?" asked the approaching cop, who simultaneously flipped the flashlight from his hip and pointed the bulb toward Randall.

"Just fine, officer. Having a little disagreement, that's all," Randall responded, while trying to sound as leveled as possible. "My name is Randall Jenkins, and I work for the Herald. Here are my credentials."

The officer narrowed his gaze and took Randall's press pass and driver's license before stepping back to his partner. They both conferred before walking back to Randall.

"Mr. Jenkins, sorry to hold you up. But we had to check out the commotion coming from this area; you're also stopped illegally," the officer said, while still visually scanning the car's interior.

The officer then pointed to the entrance to the adjacent library's parking garage, which Randall's car had partially blocked.

Randall was momentarily struck mute by the way that Marcus seemed to miraculously recover.

"Are you okay, sir?" the officer asked again, in that way cops do when they *really* want to know if you are more than just okay.

"I'm fine; just had an argument, that's all," Randall said, nodding towards Marcus. "All is good now, though."

The officers exchanged quizzical looks, before the officer handed the credentials back to Randall.

"Well, just take it easy, Mr. Jenkins. As you know, this is a new student residential area, and they will report anything out of order," the officer said. "You check out. But please, move your car, and next time, try to handle any disagreements in a less loud fashion, okay?"

"Absolutely; and thank you, officer."

The only thing fading faster than the two Temple cops was Marcus, who, Randall now feared, was making his way to the Liacouras Center to kill Frostman.

Randall staggered to the Accord before nearly collapsing into the driver's seat; he felt his mind split into two from the pressure as he sat for what felt like days.

While Randall was shaken by the knuckle-toss with Marcus and by his threat of running to the cops with some bullshit cockamamie about how he was the killer of Streaks and Levi, it dawned on Randall that Marcus would try to pin a possible third murder on his as well.

That thought snapped Randall back to reality, as his next move boiled down to trying to intercede and somehow prevent Marcus from killing Frostman or tipping off Barron to Marcus' intentions. Or both.

Then suddenly, a calming consciousness swept over Randall, due to his settling on the third option: do nothing.

Why the fuck should I get involved, either way? Marcus is now out of the way, and I know just how to deal with him if he does show up again," Randall thought. *And if Marcus does try to make a move on Frostman, he was right that Barron will most likely be there to prevent any shit like that from happening. And shit if I care about the fate of some fuckin' Frostman. Marcus would actually be doing the world a favor if he did murk Frostman.*

Relieved and content with his decision, Randall decided to call Ivey and fill her in on the latest development before continuing his journey down Broad Street.

"Hey baby; you at the center already?"

"Nah, almost. But I wanted to call you and let you know that me and that fuckin' Marcus had it out and I had to kick his ass. We got into a crazy dust-up on Broad Street. I thought I was going to kill his ass before Temple cops showed up. Crazy, but he's through; you won't hear me bringing up his name again."

On the other end, Ivey perked up and relight the blunt she had just put out. "Oh word? You finally had enough of his shit and had to throw hands, huh? Well, you were never one to play the bullshit for too long. But did something else happen?"

"Yeah, weird shit. You know dude had the audacity to actually say that he thinks I'm the one who killed Streaks and Levi? What kind of shit is that? I told him that the cops have a better case against his ass, because he was never around when the murders actually occurred.

Man, after that shit, I told his ass to bounce. Last I seen of him was his back as he was making his was to the center."

Ivey sat silent on the phone for a few moments, long enough for her to take an elaborate pull on the blunt.

"Baby, fuck that show tonight. Why don't you just come on back to my apartment? Make up some story to tell Josephine. Now I'm with you, about feeling that's some weird shit is going to go down tonight, and I don't want you anywhere near it."

Randall knew that Ivey was most likely right, but he also knew that he would need a very good reason to satisfy Josephine. And deep inside, Randall did have a level of professionalism he strove to maintain.

"Baby, as good as that sounds, I don't think I can just blow off tonight's thing. But I'll make a deal with you: I'll break out as soon as the competition portion is over. Luckily, the battle kicks off the set tonight, so I can be done earlier than later. But I won't stick around; I'll B-line it directly to you."

Ivey resisted the urge to escalate the issue and demand that Randall dip on tonight's event and just head straight to her place. But Ivey also knew that Randall's job represented a baseline principle, and it would take a major and real reason for Randall to flake on coverage.

Ivey quickly decided to not argue the point further with Randall, but she also wouldn't let it go in her mind.

Especially the part about Marcus running to Barron with his bizarro-world story that Randall somehow committed these murders. That brought back to Ivey the sense that Barron would in fact focus his full attention on making Randall out to be the perpetrator.   To Ivey, that seemed like the next logical step, as she recalled how the detective acted when he brought them down to the Roundhouse for "unofficial" questioning.

Ivey tried to remain calm, but she couldn't shake the vibe that this could end up as real trouble for Randall.

"Okay; but do me a favor? If and when you do see Detective Wilkinson, approach him before he approaches you," Ivey said. "It would probably be better if you told him everything you know about Marcus. Dude has been a drag on you ever since you met him, and it's not like you're diming him out to 5-0. And besides, if he really is guilty of committing these murders, then you wouldn't cover for him, anyway."

Randall knew Ivey made a solid point, as Randall did place a high value on self-preservation.

"You're right. Maybe seeking out Barron should be my first order of business tonight. Thanks, baby; I'll call you when this thing is over."

Ivey sat there for a few minutes to burn down the blunt and contemplate the conversation she just had with Randall.

Between puffs, Ivey allowed the competing thoughts either of going down to the center to meet Randall or just staying put at her place to duel in her mind.

She knew it was sound advice for her to just stay home and let Randall do what he had to do. *After all, there's not much I can do,* Ivey reasoned to herself. *Even if I get down there and do catch up to Randall, then what? Why do I tell him I'm there, when he asked me not to go?*

Ivey also thought of Randall's mental state. She knew he was under immense pressure, and this entire episode with Barron, Marcus and the murders had to be wearing on him.

While not directly mentioning any of this to Randall, Ivey has noticed a continued change in Randall's behavior and emotional responses.

Ivey sighed and accessed her cell between puffs and thoughts of Randall's predicament.

It was not that his behavior suddenly changed; if someone had just met Randall, they wouldn't necessarily thing anything was wrong with him or that Randall wasn't centered.

Randall always laughed it off whenever Ivey did question his odd behavior, such as the times she has witnessed Randall talking to himself in the mirror, and the times when he would get so angry that he would seem another person.

That thought struck Ivey as well. For Randall, Ivey had come to realize, was not well mentally.

Over and over again, she pleaded with him to do everything from taking a sabbatical from work to outright changing professions altogether.

Ivey knew that Randall's numerous beats and obligations were starting to wear on him.

And Ivey also noticed darker ticks in Randall's personality lately. Ivey also knew that although Randall has grown a thick skin over his years of being a reporter and from his years of growing up in West Philly, he was growing tired of absorbing all the slings and arrows from the community if a story didn't come out exactly to their liking or at the time of their choosing, as if Randall had an actual control over either issue.

Ivey shook her head and chuckled to herself when she recalled one of Randall's favorite phrases: no good deed goes unpunished.

Indeed, Randall has taken an unfair share of hate for only trying to cover the community he loved. For that, eh has received everything from hate mail to outright death threats.

And knew that some of that came with the territory, but the death threats were a whole new level of real for Randall, and it was an incident that changed Randall forever.

Ivey sat back in her lounger and took a puff as she recalled that fateful day.

Randall was working at the newsroom and bending over backwards trying to push a story through the features department about a group of rappers trying to establish an anti-crime initiative.

Randall, doing what he often did, linked the story to some city council members who were behind it.

But instead go getting a thanks and a pat-on-the-back for a job well done, one of the promoters called Randall and outright threatened to shoot him on sight. All over the promoter's name not being mentioned specifically in the article.

Randall, baffled, hurt and feeling highly disrespected on several levels, promised himself right then and there to stop giving a shit about these rappers, these community organizations, everybody. Randall also vowed to remind that promoter of where *he* was from, the next time he saw him.

Any Ivey would never forget what came next, as she literally had to talk Randall out of arming himself from then on. Randall was feet away from entering Lock's Philadelphia Gun Exchange to cop a little .32 snub-nose before Ivey was able to convince him not to make that purchase.

After all, Ivey knew that Randall never underestimated any man's threat, especially after being involved in a gunfight in his late teens.

But the incident with the promoter only stoked Randall's boiling animus toward these rappers he was forced to now cover.

But Instead of just focusing on the rhyme style, phonetic pattern and verbiage of the emcees he was covering, Randall began taking them to task for *what* they were saying.

Randall was now pointing out the hypocritical nature of their rhymes, taking them to task for their misogynist verses and blasting them for their fake gangsterism and empty materialism.

And after staring down the promoter who was made to apologize, Randall felt it was his duty to call out these culture imposters.

Oh, you've got a Benz? Randall wanted to see him whipping it.

Oh, you've got cake? Randall wanted to see him bang out that bankroll.

Oh, you've got hammers? Randall all but begged these rappers to produce that 9-millimeter.

Oh, you've got bitches? Half these rappers couldn't pull a dime from a quarter, Randall often mused to Ivey, and the other half were ducking ass-ugly baby mommas.

And if any of these street rappers actually did have those things they rhymed about, Randall was convinced it was attained through the drug game, a conclusion that only fueled Randall's contempt.

Randall's problem was that he was now saying those things out loud and putting them in print, which drew the ire of many wannabe hard street emcees throughout the city.

Randall would openly roll his eyes whenever he heard emcee so-and-so talk about the money he had, the car he drove, how many bodies he had on his hammer, and Randall's favorite - how many chicks he fucked.

True indeed, Randall's new "fuck it" attitude had sharpened over the past several months.

It also didn't escape Ivey that Randall seemed to almost take the killer's side, often saying that these rappers only got what was coming to them in the end. After all, these rappers were killed in a method akin to their lyrical persona; Ivey and Randall knew as much, and Detective Wilkinson told them as much.

But Ivey became extremely worried when Randall began saying that Streaks and Levi deserved their gruesome fate.

Randall seemed to speak with a tone of admiration when discussing the killings itself, reasoning that they each had it coming, and the murderer actually did the world a favor.

Dabbing out the blunt, those thoughts, all tied together, led Ivey to think what was unthinkable just a week ago:

Is it possible that Randall is actually the killer?

The thought made Ivey shudder and completely blew her high.

Free-spirited but supremely analytical, Ivey quietly played the role of armchair investigator as the case unfolded and enveloped everyone.

It was true that Randall has been at the scene of these two murders. But Ivey also knew that there have been other shootings at other hip-hop venues. And besides, Ivey reasoned to herself, it could all just be happenstance that Randall was assigned to cover events where these murders eventually took place.

And these were only but two entries in the very long log of killings in Philadelphia.

Ivey sucked her teeth, mad at herself for even thinking that Randall could somehow be wrapped up in these murders.

Instead of thinking of ways that Randall could be involved, Ivey focused instead on how it would be impossible for Randall to commit these murders.

For one thing, Ivey doubted that Randall had the sheer physical strength to kill Streaks, not with the way the news reported the way Streaks' killer strangled and nearly decapitated him.

And for another thing, Randall's overall temperament and visibility prevented such an act. As much as Randall hated it, everyone *knew* him or of him, from his relative local celebrity driven by his byline. Ivey had a hard time imagining a well-known and respected journalist committing such grisly crimes.

The buzzing of her cell phone jolted Ivey back to real-time.

It was Ivey's Uber driver, letting her know he was outside.

*****

GOING against his inclination, Randall knew what he had to do.

Now heading straight for the Liacouras Center, Randall's sole objective was to find Detective Wilkinson and tell him everything he knows about Marcus - the way he looks, talks, acts, and more importantly, how he confessed to killing Streaks and Levi, and that he planned on killing Frostman at tonight's event.

After dashing thoughts on calling Barron on his cell to fill him in, Randall parked in the media lot and made his way through security, which seemed particularly tight. After being shown the direction by event staff, Randall then circled around the inner access hallway that leads to the green room and stage area.

Randall felt a sudden sense of urgency in finding Barron, as he was certain now that Marcus would indeed go through with his plot to kill Frostman.

As he continued to snake his way through the bowels of the Liacouras Center, Randall contemplated on exactly how Marcus could pull of his murderous act.

With security being super thick and with the added attention provided by the Philadelphia police, it was hard for Randall to imagine any way in which Marcus could pull off the murder and get away with it. Then Randall thought that maybe, perhaps, Marcus didn't intend to get away with it at all, which he then connected back to Marcus' threat of pinning Frostman's impending murder on Randall.

Hastening his step, Randall emerged from the sunken inner bowel of the center to the back of the main staging area, which lead to the dressing rooms, greenroom and stage.

The scene was a madhouse.

Expecting just a few artists and a handful of security guards backstage, Randall was struck by how filled the area was with more than 100 self-important types.

Randall recognized straightaway the pair of uniformed and armed officers, and it was easy to spot the extra pair of plainclothes officers.

Straining his eyes, Randall slowly scanned the sea of eyes for the pair that belonged to either Barron or Marcus, hoping to spot the latter before the former. Because for Randall, seeing Barron first meant that he still had time to thwart Marcus' plan; seeing Marcus first could only mean that he was one step closer to murking Frostman.

A few local producers intercepted Randall's thoughts and line of sight by shoving their latest demos in his hand and glad-handing him to death. When he resumed his survey, Randall noticed an unmistakable pair of eyes lock on him.

Time seemed frozen still as Randall watched those eyes get closer and closer. Randall took a long, hard blink before opening his eyes.

The eyes he were following were now in his personal space, and Randall couldn't believe who it was.

"Hey baby. Surprised to see me? Don't be mad; I figured you could use the company."

Randall was momentarily immobilized by the Ivey's appearance. Randall's emotions all mixed to form a wicked concoction of anger and relief; Randall fought to keep the emotion in check.

"Sweetie, what are you doing here? You worry about me too much," Randall said over the din of the growing crowd, knowing better than to try to put Ivey on blast for not listening to him. "But maybe it's a good thing you're here. After that dust-up with Marcus, I definitely decided to come here to pull Detective Barron's coat to what Marcus is up to. Maybe you can help me find one or the other."

Randall had other shit to think about concurrently, including how he was going to pull off covering this event, regardless if he found Barron, Marcus, neither or both. Knowing the paper how he did, Randall was sure the editors would somehow spin his involvement, no matter how limited and remote it may be, into a salacious front-page story. In a blink, Randall could visualize the headline: "Our Man's First-Hand Account of the Investigation of a String of Local Rap Killings."

The thought made Randall shudder and his stomach spasm.

Randall decided right then and there to forgo covering the show and instead focused on finding Barron and stopping Marcus. At any rate, this would be a better story to sell than some rather random rap show, Randall concluded.

Dipping to a dark corner, Randall and Ivey both looked for Detective Wilkinson, while Randall also made sure to keep one eye out for Marcus.

"Maybe I should go look out front for the detective," Ivey said, now standing on the tips of her toes, trying to peer over the heads of the swelling backstage crowd. "Shit babe, he might not even come back this far."

Just as Randall turned to agree with her, Ivey vised his arm and pulled him closer.

But just as Ivey's eyes widened, as did Randall's, because this was the second time withing 20 minutes that he locked eyes with a very familiar pair of pupils.

"Randall, there's Barron. He's right over there by left exit door."

Ivey was pointing and trying to get Randall's attention, but he was consumed by the figure in the black leather hipster jacket who was burning a hole through Randall's face with his robotic, menacing stare which broke into a ghastly smile.

It was Marcus.

Randall then had the damnedest thought, that somehow left him oddly crestfallen:

Oh well; I guess Frostman will live to see another day.

Randall didn't feel the usual pang of consciousness when he previously had such cool thoughts about the killing or near-miss attempt on a person or public figure that Randall deemed had it coming.

In truth, Randall had long since rectified his distant feeling when certain individuals were killed with the overwhelming heart wrenching anguish he would feel when a "good guy" was murdered.

To Randall, there was and remained a clear distinction between the two, and he wasn't about to let those two principles interfere with one another. And the more Randall thought about it, he realized that he didn't really give a shit about Frostman's demise and didn't necessarily care if Marcus was the culprit.

But what Randall did care about was clearing his name as soon as possible and freeing himself from this bullshit.

Ivey's tightening grip snapped Randall out of his thoughts, and she began pulling Randall in Barron's direction. Randall actually felt relieved to see Barron.

Detective Wilkinson looked relieved as well, because he shot them a polite nod and began making his way toward them through the crowd.

"Detective Wilkinson. Can we talk? I have something interesting to tell you," Randall said, looking at Barron, but really looking behind and beyond him, for any sign of Marcus.

Well, I didn't expect this, Barron thought as he first shook Randall's hand, then Ivey's. *Somehow, I don't think this is going to be a confession.*

"What's on your mind, Mr. Jenkins?"

Just as Randall was about to respond, he noticed what appeared to be the back of a familiar leather jacket sliding through a closing side door.

Randall sighed. *It's time.*

"Detective Wilkinson, I know who your killer is."

Chapter Ten

DETECTIVE Barron Wilkinson couldn't believe his ears.

Wanting to be exactly sure of what Randall was saying, he ushered the pair through a secured doorway which led to the main sound room, which doubled as Barron's on-scene headquarters for his operation.

The room, aside from being the digital brain of the entire audio and video operation for the evening, also provided a panoramic view of the greenroom area directly below.

From there, Barron, Ivey and Randall could talk in relative privacy while keeping an eye on the quasi-celebrities and their assembled hangers-on.

Ivey, having spun a few sets here, was familiar with the layout and seemed very comfortable as she plopped down in the engineer's chair.

Randall, however, has never ventured neither into the bowels of the Liacouras Center nor the entertainment command center in which all three were now sitting in.

Ivey's icy stare never left Barron's face, who was wearing the mug of a detective both on the verge of solving a major case and totally unsure of what he was about to hear next.

Randall, his mind trying to put together the proper string of words that would make most sense to the detective, instead found himself strangely tripping over his tongue.

"Detective Wilkinson, what can I say? You were right. Marcus. That's the name of the person you are looking for, the person I know is behind these killings.

"And I think he's going to make a try for Frostman tonight."

The room feel deathly silence, save for the din of the repetitive baseline being pushed out by the state-of-the-art A/V system.

It was quiet enough to hear the stares. Barron staring at Randall; Randall staring at Barron, and Ivey now staring at the both of them, in what looked like a still from a silent movie's Mexican Standoff scene.

Barron instantly thought Randall was serving him a steaming pile of bullshit.

After what seemed like an eternity, Barron's face morphed into a sarcastic smirk.

"Is that right? And why should I believe you?" Barron asked in a manner that dripped with incredulity. "You must be pretty close to this Marcus to know his next move."

As Barron folded his arms across his chest and leaned back on the engineer's table, the unsaid implication was clear: that to Barron, Randall always had this information and decided not to tell the detective, until now.

Randall sighed. *Fuck it.*

"Look, detective, this is going to sound crazy, but hear me out. This guy, Marcus, rolls up on me Saturday morning while I was eating breakfast at Two Boots. He made some smart-ass comment about my music selection and we just sort of struck up a conversation," Randall said. "He said he was new to the area, and interested in the local hip-hop scene, and I told him about the upcoming shows.

"He wanted to check them out, and although I didn't want to hang out with him, I obliged and met him at the show where Streaks was killed. We then linked up for the show, where Levi was killed.

After that, I sort of began it put one and one together, but at that point, Marcus had already told me straight-up that he killed the two, and that he was going to murk Frostman tonight."

Randall was sweating and breathless after his retelling.

While both Barron and Ivey stood in static, Barron wore the look of someone who just had his intelligence questioned.

"And?" Barron finally said.

"And what? That's about it," Randall said, knowing that for Detective Wilkinson, that was hardly *it*.

"Randall, you're wasting my time. What you told me sounds like you just made it up on the spot, and this ain't no freestyle cipher," Barron said in a mocking manner. "You're going to have to give me something much, much better than that if you want me to take you seriously…and if you want to truly remove yourself from my prime suspect list."

Randall locked eyes with the detective, who was now close enough that Randall could smell his breath.

"So….and?"

At that moment, Randall had the damnedest thought: he never did get to know Marcus' last name. Randall them wondered how Marcus could seem so familiar yet know so little about him.

"Well, I can also provide you with a physical description, and sort of his mannerisms, Randall said. His about my height, but a little taller; a little huskier than me and seems to wear clothes a size too big for him. And he also has this slice on the right side of his face, going from above his eyebrow, straight down his eyelid and down to face."

That last note seemed to grab at least a little of the Barron's attention. Still, the detective knew he had Randall on his heels, and he was determined to pump Randall for every drop of information he could.

"So, let me get this straight: some guy you don't know, and whom you only have a vague description of, confides in you that he is a serial killer? Why doesn't that work for me?" Barron said. "Right now, you don't have anything close to motive to put on this so-called Marcus, and even if you did, it's only your word saying that he was even at those venues, let alone killed those two rappers.

"What can I do with that?"

Barron leaned back to give Randall some room to digest the exchange.

"Well, if Randall is right, then Marcus will make a play for Frostman, right?" Ivey said, breaking the dead-air standoff. "So that means he is either here or will be. Detective, Randall gave you a good rundown of what he looks like - that scar should be enough of an identifying feature, no? Then maybe we should just look for this guy, and if you happen to find him, then he can answer all of our questions."

Barron actually thought that was a halfway decent plan, but it still had lots of logistical holes. And Barron certainly wasn't going to let the pair know just how good of an idea it was.

Still, it would be hard to spot a scarred face among the throng of attendees, many of whom who probably had a scar similar to the one Randall described.

Barron, in lending more weight to the situation, radioed in a be-on-the-lookout alert to his team for anyone matching the description Randall provided.

"He may have a gun and wearing black gloves," Randall blurted out, wishing instantly that he didn't.

Barron rolled his eyes while Ivey shot Randall an exasperated gesture.

However, Barron didn't relay that bit of info to his team. Perhaps they already assumed Marcus was armed, so no need to waste precious seconds with that bit.

Barron turned back to Randall and a now-standing Ivey.

"Now before we get down to catching this Marcus, if he is even here tonight, I need to know how you can be so sure that he is going to try to kill Frostman? Does he have a problem with this person?"

Randall signed. It was time to tell the tale.

"Because he told me that was his plan," Randall said. "Look detective, I know this sounds crazy, but I'm telling you, this dude Marcus means business. About two hours ago, him and I got into a tussle on Diamond Street after he hipped me to his plan," Randall said. "Right after that, I got here as quick as I could to get in touch with you and let you know.

"I didn't have to do that; but I know I owed it to you, and I want this guy caught just as much as everyone else does. He's fucking up things for everybody."

Just then, a group of engineers entered the room, and paused for a minute when they encountered the trio.

Barron introduced himself and presented his badge before assuring the engineers there was nothing going on beside a routine security check.

The engineers were setting up for the main spectacle, which was Frostman's highly-customized intro.

Once outside the room, Barron guided the pair downstairs and through another secured door that led to a row of unfurnished meeting spaces.

The rooms were cavernous, and Randall felt that he could breathe for the first time in a long time.

"So now what?" Ivey said.

"Look Randall, this is as far as you and Ivey go with this. I want the both of you to stay here while we look for this Marcus of yours," Barron said matter-of-factly. "If he is here, and if he is as cunning as you think he is, then if he spots either of you, you're liable to goose him into doing something even more unpredictable. This way, I know you're safe in here.

"And if he isn't here, then I know exactly where you two will be in case I need to ask you some further questions."

Being unofficially locked up didn't at all sit well with Ivey, while Randall didn't seem to mind it as much.

"So, detective, are we your prisoners now? What jurisdiction do you have to possibly hold us," demanded Ivey.

Now it was Barron's turn to break out in a smile.

"And miss all this excitement? Of course, you aren't under any sort of hold or arrest, and are free to leave at any time," Barron said. "But something tells me both of you would rather be here than anywhere else right now. Who knows? Think of it as me keeping you safe from harm. If Marcus has zero compunction in terms of killing two rappers and making a bold play on a third, there's no telling what he would do to either of you if he had a chance."

Randall could see the tension in Ivey's body language give way to a sense of understanding resentment as she sighed and leaned up against the wall.

"We will do it your way, detective," Ivey said as Randall nodded in agreement. "For now."

With that, Barron barked another order into his radio and left the room. When the security door clicked, it let out a reassuring electronic whir that relayed that no one was getting in nor out of that room without direct access.

"Well, shit. It's all in Barron's hands now," Randall said, half pleased and half exhausted. In a way, Randall was actually happy to be in the room, because if Marcus did somehow manage to kill Frostman or be captured somewhere in the act, it would instantly free Randall of any culpability.

Ivey was now sitting on the floor with her back to the wall and her knees unto her chin.

"Baron is gonna blow it and somehow blame you," Ivey said in the dead-ass manner she uses when resigned to a certain outcome. "He doesn't believe you. He'll say some shit about your description being too vague and that there is no way Marcus nor anyone else will be able to even get close enough to Frostman tonight to kill him.

"And even if Marcus does, there's no way he can get out of here without getting caught. And then Barron will blame you for adding and abetting, after-the-fact."

Fuck my life, instantly ran through Randall's mind.

"Ivey, if Barron finds Marcus, this shit is all over, for all the reasons you've just said. I don't care what Barron has to say after that," Randall said. "I just want this shit to be over with. Tonight."

Just then, Ivey's face brightened, and she stood up like a bolt.

"Well, if we want out of here and want to help Barron avoid a major fuck-up, we can't do it from here," Ivey said, whipping out her iPhone.

*****

JUST then, the sound system became noticeably louder and the bass became deeper, which only meant that the engineers had queued up the start of Frostman's rather gaudy entrance.

In sort of a mixture between Isaac Hayes' *Soul Train* entrance and a pimper's parade, Frostman recited his latest hit while walking to the stage on a bed of red rose petals, breezily laid in front of him by a harem of eight scantily clad junoesque women.

The crowd ate it up.

Barron kept a keen eye on the backstage area as Frostman zipped through his performance, which was laden with pimp-talk and references to everyone from Iceberg Slim and Goldie to Reverend Ike and Ice-T.

Barron was relieved that Frostman's show ended without alarm or distraction. Although his men haven't seen anyone fitting Marcus' description, they were able to provide the extra layer of security the detective hoped for. All that was left was for Frostman to make it backstage and out of the arena, and then the immediate area, and Barron could then disqualify Randall's theory, which in turn would allow the detective to really turn up the heat on his favorite reporter.

Randall seethed and felt himself boiling on the inside when he heard Frostman's lyrics and the fans' reaction. Randall just couldn't fathom how thousands of fans would pay good money to see someone spew such blatant misogynistic lyrics that included referred to women as whores, bitches, sluts and every other despicable thing.

It agitated Randall further as his mind projected an image of the crowd filled with many of the women who looked just like the ones Frostman rapped about. Randall was dumbfounded that Frostman could say all of these things, and worse, be promoted by radio, the internet and by mindless fans as the next big thing out of Philly.

Fuck it, Randall thought to himself. *Marcus would be doing the world a favor if he killed this motherfucker. That would be one less corny voice out there, drowning out the real hip-hop the world isn't hearing because of punk-ass rappers like Frostman.*

Ivey's phone call snapped Randall from his searing inner rage.

"I know, right? The detective must've accidentally locked the door behind himself when he was done showing Randall and I around. I never saw this part of the Liacouras Center before," Ivey said. "So, you can come down and open this door for us? My man. Name the song you want me to play, and I'll shout you out next week."

Ivey beeped off the phone call and looked at Randall with the look of mischievous, clue-sniffing cat.

"So, you wanna smoke this before Cooper lets us out?" Ivey said, producing a spliff and lighter from her small carryall. "We should have a few minutes, at least; he's just wrapping up the handoff for the rest of the show."

What Randall didn't know was that Ivey recognized one of the engineers that came up to the soundroom as one of her good friends on the deejaying circuit, and Ivey remembered they had exchanged numbers a few months ago so they could team up on a gig. Ivey was playing it off like her and Randall were locked in the room by mistake.

Ivey smiled. Randall did the opposite.

"I love you, but are you fuckin' crazy? We leave now, and like this, Barron is really going to suspect me of murking these rappers. This is not a good idea, Ivey," Randall said.

Ivey calmly lit the flared end of the spliff and took one long puff. Holding it, she then exhausted a slow stream of whitish grey smoke away from the direction of the smoke alarms.

"Randall, and I love you too, but it's time you man the fuck up and take control of this situation," Ivey said while passing Randall the spliff. "For far too long, you've let too many people dictate your moves and thoughts to you. I say fuck that; it's time for you to take charge of your own movements and your own destiny, starting now.

"Fuck what Barron says. What, he's going to lock us up because he's mad at us? You heard him; we are free to go whenever we like. And I'd like to see him try, because I would slap him with an unlawful detention suit quicker than he can think."

Randall both resented and admired Ivey's tone, because she was right. But it's not what she said, it's how she said it.

But after taking two pulls on the spliff, Randall's anger of Ivey's tone diminished, he understood her rationalization. The pair could do little more in here than being a side dish for the detective if he couldn't bag his main course.

Randall was always amazed at how a toke or two could calm him down just enough to take the starch out of any situation he encountered. And Ivey knew that well about him, which is why she seemed to have an endless supply of marijuana at the ready and at all times while she was with Randall.

By the time Cooper made it downstairs to spring Ivey and Randall, the pair had all but finished the spliff and were on the same accord: together, they were going to look for Marcus in the crowd. Just because Frostman's performance was over didn't mean that Marcus wouldn't make a play for him out in the open.

"Thanks, Coop; this door should have some kind of anti-lock feature," Ivey said as the pair emerged from the room. "How was the show?"

Cooper and Ivey exchanged brief small talk before Cooper darted back up to the soundroom.

"So, I guess our next step is to check out the Broad Street entrance; if we know Frostman, we know he'll most likely be out front, soaking up his fandom before he, his Lincoln and his hoes dip off into the night."

Randall smiled at Ivey's play on words.

"I suppose so. But what if Barron sees us?" Randall said.

"So? What he's going to do besides look really hard at us," Ivey said. "We will tell him the truth; that an engineer needed the room and told us to get out."

Randall was amazed at Ivey's ever-devious mind.

The pair circled the bowl behind the soundroom and emerged from the stairwell directly to the left and below the stage.

They ran down the leftmost isle to blend in with the last of the exiting patrons who were piling out onto Broad Street.

Randall engorged his lungs on the crisp night air as the he and Ivey emerged out onto the concrete apron of the center. As if she could tell the future, Ivey was right: there was Frostman, in all his pimp glory, talking to fans while surrounded by all of his women.

Randall didn't know if it was because everyone had on Timberlands, but he had a hard time seeing over the heads and shoulders of the crowd.

Ivey seemed to be having the same issue.

"Maybe we should split up?" Ivey said. "You definitely know what he looks like, and I have a good idea."

Speaking of ideas, Randall didn't think this was a good one either, but again, he could see Ivey's rationalization. And Randall sincerely wouldn't be able to ever forgive himself if Marcus' spotted Ivey *before* she saw him and is able to alert either himself or Barron.

Reluctantly, Randall agreed, and the pair split up and began to circumnavigate swelling crowd.

As he sidestepped through the crowd and tried to avoid any chitchat with the many emcees, producers and deejays he knew, Randall noticed a thrilling sensation rumble through his being as he managed to get closer to Frostman. It was sort of an odd, anticipatory feeling that made Randall's mouth water.

Randall's footsteps began to slow, as did time itself, as his thoughts veered from finding Marcus to wondering what Marcus was going to do to Frostman.

Even more, Randall thought of what he himself would like to do to this pimp rapper if given the opportunity.

Randall salivated at the thought of administering to Frostman, in the most unpleasant fashion imaginable, the pain that he has inflicted on so many young girls and women.

Randall allowed a grim smile to curl his lips as he thought of sodomizing Frostman with many of the sex toys he rhymed about and often bought on stage to use as props.

Randall delighted in the vision of Frostman's manhood being hacked off and feed to him, while his heart pumped when he conjured the fluorescent imagery of Frostman's mangled lower intestine, burst and exposed, leaking from his torn and exploded rectum.

Randall felt woozy from the orgasmic rush provided by the mental imagery.

An afterglow short-lived, as his mind was drawn back to by the sight of an all-to-familiar fit: brown Timberlands, dark blue jeans and a black leather hipster. A look that was tied together by a long scar down the face.

Marcus smiled.

Randall seemed to be miles away from him, and the closer he got to him, the further Marcus seemed to be moving away from the crowd.

Picking up the pace and not knowing what exactly he would do if he did confront Marcus for the second time this evening, Randall broke into a half-jog and followed Marcus down the steps of the Center and towards Cecil B. Moore Avenue.

On the other side of the crowd, Barron too was surveying the crowd, after he emerged from the Center, and thought for a moment that he spotted someone who could possibly fit the description provided by Randall.

On the verge of ending what so far has been a fruitless, if uneventful operation, Barron's eyes then locked on a pair of almond-shaped eyes that were staring back at him in muted alarm.

It was Ivey.

But Ivey wasn't looking at Barron; she was looking beyond him at a rather quick-moving Randall.

Ivey was stopped by the very angry detective before she could reach the sidewalk to go after Randall.

"I thought I told you and Randall to stay inside until I let you out," Barron boomed. "You and your reporter boyfriend are going to jeopardize this operation and your own safety."

Ivey was unmoved as she looked to aside from Barron to see in which direction Randall headed.

In breathless fashion, Ivey told Barron that she just saw Randall leaving, and it looked like he was in hurry.

"And if you want to talk to Randall and maybe even catch Marcus, we need to catch up to him, and we need to catch up to him right now."

With that, Ivey leapt down the Center's front steps and ran toward Cecil B. Moore. Once there, Ivey figured that Randall must've turned toward 15th street, and she made a sharp right and continued her chase.

Barron was hot on her heels and not knowing exactly what to expect; the detective was also juggling his radio, dispatching his team to the intersection of 17th and Cecil B. Moore. What little Ivey was able to hear sounded like Barron was giving his team the description of Randall instead of Marcus.

No wanting to stop to clarify with Barron as to why Randall was now the person of interest, Ivey continued running until reaching a cross street. There; she paused to catch her breath, and had apparently lost her escort, as she looked back and couldn't make out Barron from the dark shadows and poor lighting from a cracked overhead streetlight that splayed out an eerie, blackish-orange glow.

Momentarily disoriented even though she was only two blocks away from the Center, Ivey slowed to walk and squinted her eyes to adjust to the darkness.

Ivey's already tense nerves almost snapped from the strain of her jumping out of her skin at the sound of three gunshots licked off in succession. The unmistakable sound of gunplay filled her heart with dread, as she could only think of Randall's safety.

Oh no, Randall! Please god, don't let it be him.

Now running down 17th Street toward where she thought the gunshots came from, Ivey almost fainted on the spot at the sight of a body face down on the sidewalk, bleeding from three bullet holes in the upper back.

It was Detective Barron Wilkinson.

Ivey lips mutely pounded together as she was struck frozen by the sight and condition of the wounded officer. Gathering up the will, Ivey reached for her iPhone with both of her trembling hands.

Ivey felt the wind leave her lungs and had trouble catching her breath as she tapped out "911" on her phone's screen.

"911. What is your emergency?"

"I think…Detective Wilkinson has been shot," Ivey stammered out, her chest and head now ponding and her whole being shuddering. "He's at…he's at…."

"…He's at the corner of 17th and Burks," said a calm voice behind Ivey, which made her turn and drop her phone.

To be continued…

www.ingramcontent.com/pod-product-compliance
Ingram Content Group UK Ltd.
Pitfield, Milton Keynes, MK11 3LW, UK
UKHW051119030625
6205UKWH00040B/815